AF436783

I AM KARATE

Printed in Argentina - Printed in Argentina
Tapas design: Gerardo R. Ahumada
DTP: Raúl E. Ahumada
Printing and Binding: Independent publisher.
©2018 - First Edition
ISBN 978-987-42-9889-8
Deposit No. 712523 of 26 September 2018.
Córdoba – Republic Argentina
Suggestions and comments to the author: reahumada@yahoo.com

I AM KARATE

The legend of Itosu Anko

Raúl Ahumada

*I dedicate this book
to the memory of my
beloved parents...*

INDEX

PREFACE

With great pleasure I finally conclude the story, or rather the legend, which is reflected in the pages of this book.

A novel full of emotions, which collects and gathers many of the teachings and stories that this great master of the style of karate-do Shorin Ryu had to live.

Itosu Anko expressed in the continuity of the lineage that gave him, his Master Matsumura Sokon, the principles of good reputation that formed his martial training.

Nobody who knows his life, could reasonably deny that he dedicated himself to art with dedication and, above all, very service-oriented. Thanks to his effort, karate was incorporated into the teaching of Okinawa schools, which also gave him a strong diffusion impulse.

It was not easy to obtain a detailed explanation of the biography of the master Itosu. In a recent conversation with Master Tsuha Kiyoshi Hanshi, who is an authority on the history of Okinawan karate, he said that unfortunately there is very little information about this great martial artist.

It is only recently that they began to show photographic images of him person and they are the ones reproduced on the cover of this text.

Although it is a novel and i have used fiction into the history, the thread of the narrative responds to a consistency such that its reading will surely be pleasant and entertaining. Not only for those who practice or like martial arts, but also for those who do not know anything about them.

Also, as always, i wish thanks to all those anonymous contributors who with their publications contributed to this work could be edited.

As well, i wish the reader for patience in case there was an unintentional translation error, because the original work was written in Spanish and it was a challenge to show it in English too.

Finally, I want to express special thanks to the people of Okinawa and all their karate's Master whom I admire and respect. Thank you very much!

INTRODUCTION

Between 1832 and 1915 the fruitful life of a great master of the Shorin Ryu style of karate-do took place. Great among the greats, his name was Itosu Anko...

Here is his legend...

CHAPTER 1

KISHI BUSHI

The old master had been taking a little *ryokucha* (green tea) before going to bed. The cup that contained it trembled in his callused hands. His tired and leisurely step gave clear account of the years already lived. It was March of the year 1915 on the island of Okinawa. The winter was coming to an end and he could feel the penetrating and fresh aroma of the first *sakura*[1] flowers. The sun shone as always, caressing at that hour with its warm rays the meekness of the afternoon.

It was then that he said to himself: *<This has always been my favorite season>*.

That in which he performed the *hanami*[2], especially with

---

[1] The cherry blossoms of Okinawa are called *'kanhi zakura',* and they are *sakuras* that bloom in winter. They need a little cold to bloom. Excerpted from: http://unajaponesaenjapon.com/43240/las-primeras-flores-del-sakura-2018-en-okinawa-japon

[2] It literally means "to look at the flowers" (*Hana*-flor *Mi*-mirar) and refers to the "contemplation of the beauty of the flower".

the arrival of spring.

He said to himself: <*Look at the cherry trees flowering has also taught me an important lesson: this flower is of a very ephemeral life, but nevertheless during that short period of time, nothing prevents it from showing its exuberance, delivering its fragrance and its great beauty.*

And that is what every human being should seek. Like this little flower, living in fullness giving the world the best we have to give. Without worrying or thinking that life happens very fast and soon we become memories. Memories that will always be endearing, depending on how much "fragrance" we have scattered throughout life>

He meditated on this revealing thought, while he was looking at the wood on the ceiling of his room. He was breathing slowly and had covered part of his body with a blanket, because at times he felt an inexplicable current of coldness overtake him and produce an uncomfortable tremor.

It was not a dream what he felt, but nevertheless he could not stay fully awake. Then he asked himself: <*What strange feeling is this?* >

He did not find any meaning in the perceptions that invaded him. Trembling even if it was not cold, a dream that he could not control and that also led him to close his eyes with increasingly long and spaced blinks. In that stupor he began to feel that nothing around him was in place. Suddenly, as if his body did not belong to him, he awoke to observe his reclining figure from another perspective. He no longer felt that unpleasant feeling of cold and there was no tremor in him either. A very white light occupied all the space of the room and in that moment different passages of his life were present as a whirlpool. He understood that he was facing end point of the road. But he had already learned from his masters that this day was coming and he was ready for that.

He evoked nostalgic the lesson received by his beloved master Matsumura Sokon who said goodbye to the earthly life with a smile on his old lips. He could still remember the peace with which he found it on his face that unfortunate day he died, almost twenty years ago. And now he was fighting that final battle himself. But he was also a warrior, though a warrior of peace. During the long apprenticeship of Art, his *Sensei* had advised him to harden his hands and limbs, but without losing sight of the importance of cultivating his spirit. Now he heard clearly the words he gave him one afternoon after the intense and daily practice:

—*Dear Anko, you must always remember that although you can have powerful hands, the nobility must always live in your heart. I'm going to give you a gift that will be contained in the slogan: Kishi Bushi, that is to say devil's hands and spirit of Buddha. I want you to meditate on it and apply it with honor to your whole existence.*

He was sure that he had generously fulfilled the noble inheritance given to him. His calloused and hard hands gave an account of that. However, it was not as soon as he learned to cultivate his spirit.

<*Kishi Bushi ... Kishi Bushi ...*> for a good part of his life those words resounded in his mind. However, he needed to reach maturity to understand the second part of the legacy of his beloved master.

Without knowing why, but for him it was the first thing he remembered that afternoon. The unforgettable message of whoever was his mentor and that he would keep forever in his heart.

<From this day that I will have to transpose the doors of eternity and live there forever, with my last breath I will honor the memory of my dear master Sokon. Therefore I will give my life in exchange for being in the memory of those who remember me as Kishi Bushi or as a spiritual warrior, fulfilling in it with his valuable offering.>

The *ichiban deshi* (main student) of the master Matsumura was thus preparing to transpose the doors of the other life totally at peace with his conscience, having learned to serve with loyalty to that land that saw him being born.

And what a great and faithful fulfillment with that inheritance of honor!

TEGUMI

Suddenly he saw himself as a child among the thick white fog that surrounded him. He was born in 1832 within a typical home of the Ryukyuan nobility.

At that time there were moments overwhelms due to the harsh domination exercised on the island by the Satsuma Clan. They were bloodthirsty warriors, very unfriendly and above all felt the pride of belonging to the nobility of the empire they guarded. They only had some respect for the *keimochis* (royal guards) since they were also nobles of the Ryūkyū Kingdom. And these last ones were it because they had the mission to guard and defend the king from any attack or aggression. His father had been a rigorous *Peichin*[3] and applied that rigor to every act of his life. Raising and educating him, his only son, could not be the exception to his closed martial thought. Memories carried him back to that time when he was still a child and enjoyed going through the forests of his native Okinawa. He and his friends were very motivated to observe the innumerable colors and the prodigious life that took place in those places. Pursuing locusts and organizing fights between spiders and other insects was the favorite

---

[3] The *Peichin* represented in the kingdom the equivalent of the samurai in Japan.

pastime they used to share. They were placed around a small circular corral covered with sand and about three feet in diameter. It was surrounded by a thick cord made of sun-dried mud. And there was fought between the different insects that trained as real pets. They spent whole hours watching carefully how each of them used a different modality to defend and attack. The most fearsome were the *mukade*[4] who were trained with careful dedication. He was sure that some *kabuto* (helmets) of the samurai should have been inspired by the appearance of these insects in motion to attack. It is also used in these fight, spiders or "crab" spiders, which can reach up to thirty centimeters and, although they are not characterized by being weavers, in particular the females are extremely aggressive and combative. Over the years, he understood and was sure that this could have been *Tegumi's* original spark[5]. And he said to

---

[4] This species of centipede is very aggressive and territorial. Its bite is not mortal for man but it is mortal for other insects.

[5] The catch, shock, grips and evasion techniques were used to make the attacker and bring him down in the old style of *tegumi*, which was used by the trainees to hone their skills in the predecessor

himself: <*At the end, everything comes from nature and although many truths remain hidden in it, they are also waiting to be revealed. It is man's condition to remove the veil that covers them and generously they will be shown to those who know how to interpret and respect their codes.*>

But to his father who was very impatient and strict, these practices bothered him irreparably. He used to rebuke him by saying that he would never learn how to defend a home if he spent his time on unimportant things. Then he applied penances that consisted in improving his calligraphy and learning Chinese literature.

In his home there was a library with many books of stories, legends and religion, to which he had no other option than to devote time to reading. When his father took him a lesson and he showed doubts for not having read enough, it gave him a singular punishment. Now he was making a pious pause in the story of his mind. He

---

Karate (Tode-jutsu). *Tegumi* is a term in *Hogen* native of Okinawa used to describe a plebeian form of struggle.

could not remember his father as a cruel person, although as a child he would have thought that he was. It is that in his goal of making him a strong and autonomous man he used methods that would mark him forever. The scene that came back to his mind at that moment was the following: he saw his father who was taking him to the yard of the house where there was a low tree to which a rope tied him. At the other end of the rope, he made a loop around his small waist. Then with a stick he began to run it from behind while hitting him on the buttocks with that object that measured more than one meter in length. He remembered that his escape was limited until the moment when he had so much turned around the tree, and the rope was getting shorter and tighter, until finally he left immobilized. And then, not being able to run anymore, he received a painful beating with the stick. But over the years he could learn that better than running and scaping, it was to face each blow with his hands and divert or stop them. This instead of angering his father, on the contrary it made him feel happy that he could defend himself. And on several occasions he managed to remove the stick from his hands and counterattack it with such fury that one day he finally reduced the element of martyrdom into splinters.

<Today I realize that those years prepared me for what came later. With pain I learned, but like so the sword hardens when, when leaving the forge, blows are applied with the mallet, I became a hard individual tempered in the forge of a Peichin warrior as was my noble father>

GUSUKUMA SENSEI

He continued to float weightlessly in that space around his body that was already sleeping in eternal sleep, when another memory began to be present and he said: <From this fog that surrounds me and that I can feel between my fingers like dense and soft cloud, now appears the image of my first Sensei. His name was Gusukuma>

A feeling of gratitude filled him, when suddenly he found himself facing him again in this kind of endless dream. He could not speak to him but his unmistakable figure and smiling face greeted him with great affection.

As if magically he had returned to the age of ten years of life, he could be seen behind the mist next to the old Chinese master in the courtyard of the house that he lived in the area of Tomari[6]. His influential father had taken the necessary steps to present him and to be admitted as a practitioner of the old *Tode*[7].

What he had learned from the clandestine feuds between insects and the rudimentary defenses against the blows of the rod that his father propitiated, now began to be

---

[6] Chinese teachers introduced physical exercises as a general practice for the development of health and discipline. It is a recognized fact that in Chinese culture the best medicine for all ailments is to perform breathing exercises accompanied by rhythmic movements of the body. For this philosophy, the general cause of all diseases came from inactivity. Thus, the precursors of Chinese medicine, from the most ancient antiquity had already observed the value of these practices. It is also part of this culture the fact that the best way to do physical exercises and breathing, consists of series imitating movements of different animals, but in a smooth and leisurely way.

[7] It has its origin in the indigenous martial arts of the Ryūkyū Islands, called *Te* (手, literally, "hand", or *Tii* in the local *Uchinaaguchi* dialect) and in the Chinese *kenpo*.

systematized. The first thing Gusukuma taught him was to maintain a relaxed and flexible posture.

He was a man of very few words for which he used to show his movements and told him to imitate them. In one of the sporadic times he used words instead of gestures, he said:

—*Anko must make sure that your movements are like those of the leaves of a field planted with rice. They move without offering resistance to the wind and even swirl responding to their capricious gusts. But that does not prevent that in its generous pods is maturing the germ that will end in fruit.*

The philosophy of that honorable old master was modeling not only in his body that looked stronger and more fibrous, but also his mind and spirit.

Once the different positions were happening naturally, he began with an important work on how to breathe[8] concentrated in the abdomen.

---

[8] There are basically two types of breathing: the *Kyoshiki Kokyu* (chest breathing) and the *Fukushiki Kokyu* (abdominal breathing). A very ingrained belief that in our abdomen there is an energy nucleus

All the training consisted of feeling the energy that accumulated in that vital center *(tandem)*, until little by little he verified that he could get to control it. During the years of practice with this venerable master he was able to learn to combine techniques of displacement, breathing and above all to associate his spirit with each movement. He was preparing to be a man and was advancing with dedication in his martial training.

And so, like the grain of rice and the wind, it was maturing in its interior to the vagaries of life preserving the spiritual peace and without opposing any resistance to what he will live in the future,

---

called a *tandem*. This center is not an organ, but a point at which energy accumulates and from which it is distributed throughout the body. The simplest method to accumulate energy in the *tandem* is to increase the pressure in the abdomen by performing an abdominal breathing *(Fukushiki Kokyu)*. Inhaling the air that contains mainly oxygen and nitrogen and exhaling carbon dioxide will mean that it is inspired to assimilate energy from the universe (called *Ki* in Nihongo) and it is expelled to discharge the contaminated energy produced by our own body.

With a last look of gratitude, he dismissed the master Gusukuma, who gradually disappeared after the white mist that surrounded him.

ASATO ANKO

Immediately after the image of his first *Sensei* was erased, the presence of another person who also marked his life began to reveal itself behind the thick fog. It was his great friend Asato Anko. Now he could not help but embrace that brother of the *do* (path to perfection) he died about ten years ago. His friend who was *Tonochi* (village hereditary chief) had been born in the village of Asato that was located halfway between Naha and Shuri. The destinies of both were linked by sharing the same precepts of teaching and the rigor with which they were taught. In fact, his friend also had to apply himself in letters, calligraphy and Chinese classics. It was because of this that he became a writer identifying himself as *Rinkakusai* (which means unusual and pure) as a pseudonym for his compositions and calligraphy.

Together, Asato and Itosu had diligently studied martial arts under the strict tutelage of Matsumura Sokon. The latter honored how he taught his own master Sakugawa Satunuke. The demanding instruction was always carried out very early, before dawn, without changes or taking into account any holiday period.

During that time Asato was also studying at the National School where he was an excellent student and for that reason he received an honorary scholarship. Until the moment when life reunited them, one and the other were formed in the Art of combat but in different sources. Asato who liked riding and archery had been instructed by important masters in these specialties, always standing out in each of them. But it represented more faithfully the traditions and culture of Japan, than the one that ruled in the Ryūkyū archipelago before it had been definitively assimilated by the Meiji era empire.

Now both were placed in *seiza* position kneeling one next to the other. In front of them the cloud began to clear.

This took the form of a ring several meters in diameter that surrounded an image that increased in sharpness and that both began to seem very familiar. They were seen fleeing from a crowd of thugs in one of the narrow streets of feudal Okinawa. They did not show them concern in them faces. On the contrary, they shared a complicit laugh that indicated that they had committed some mischief. Before this scene, Itosu Anko could not remain silent and then said:

—*Oh look! What a shame I feel today to see this! I realize that although we enjoyed it, they were transgressions of our immature youth.*

—*Chsss friend!* - with understanding Asato asked him to be quiet —*Nothing you can do to change what has already happened. I understand your shame, but look at our happy faces back then and enjoy what is to come. All this has been necessary and nothing in our lives has ceased to have a meaning.*

Itosu then nodded with a slight gesture, but as the scenes were reproduced at times he took his head with both hands, which made him give a spontaneous laugh to his companion in adventures. They were two mature old men who looked at each other being young and each one living it differently. Itosu did it with modesty and his dear friend Asato did it with almost irreverent humor. Meanwhile the images showed that they were quickly getting into a house in the village. Hours before this happened; his persecutors had taken them as two weak children of society. But what they did not know was what kind of martial artists they had tried to attack. An old saying holds that low-ranking people liked to copy the actions of those who belonged to a higher class. During those times there was in that village of Asato a group of brave young people but with little or no sense of morality. They often enjoyed bragging and sometimes even messed with weak or helpless passers-by beating them up. As a result, the people of Asato acquired a terrible reputation for unjustified violence. They both walked through one of its quiet streets, when suddenly they were surrounded by a mob that threatened them defiantly trying to deprive them of their few belongings. When they realized that the group of aggressors was made up of more than twenty brave-looking youth, they decided to apply some evasive strategy. At one point

Itosu pretended to fall to the floor, unconscious from the shock. This caused confusion and the leader of the group went ahead with curiosity to verify it. But he could not notice that he took advantage and took a handful of sand from the ground, which went straight to his eyes. And taking advantage of the general confusion of those, they left running away in a hurry and laughing more than could while the conceited thug scrubbed his face and roared like a caged lion.

But they were young and for them what happened was just a game. Of course, they did not think that same group of corpulent individuals and went after them to hunt them mercilessly. They thought that if they took refuge in that house they would be safe and the crowd would dissipate tired, but none of that happened. On the contrary, instead of twenty, there were forty subjects who composed the irritated entourage. They got together like wasps outside the house and kicked the door furiously demanding that they leave or that they would enter and force them out of there. Then, the most diplomatic of the two who was Asato told Itosu in that afflictive occasion: - Allow me friend to leave to convince them of their error since we have nothing valuable to deliver them. Do not worry I'm sure they'll understand. Meanwhile, you should go out the back door of the house. Itosu looked at him with unconcealed astonishment because he could not believe what his friend wanted to do. These people were not friends to talk to and they only wanted to punish them for the dishonor they had subjected to the clan's leader. But before he could comment, he saw with dread that his friend was leaving the house and closing the door behind him. The voices calmed down and he could hear how his friend spoke to the crowd, he showing correctness and diplomacy. Suddenly, the roars began again as he obeyed what his friend had indicated. Great was his surprise to see that in that sector of the house there was also a group of men who watched that exit. He had no choice but to go out and face them. He was not good to talk, as his friend Asato was, but he had learned to defend himself very well. Meanwhile, on the other front, Asato, who logically had not managed to convince the angry leader of the band of bandits with words, began to defend himself vigorously against his attacks. Dodging a circular blow that launched and dodged a few inches above his head, he launched a violent *uraken* (blow with the back of the fist) with which he literally buried his nose inside the cranial cavity. The subject fell heavily to the ground while spitting blood through his mouth. The second of the rivals prepared to attack but this time with another. But they could not even touch him because with two powerful *mae gueri* (front kick) he gave them two precise punches in the crotch area that made them fall on the ground broken and almost unable to breathe. And so the bloody fight continued, but the rivals who succeeded the former were too inexperienced and ended up with broken arms, dislocated knees and there was even one who cried out in pain so strong that no one else wanted to risk continuing the fight. Undoubtedly Asato was a terrible opponent. Physically he was broad-shouldered, muscular and had learned to use his hands and legs as if they were real spears. In that he stopped to think what would have become of his friend Anko. He hurried to the back of the house without knowing what he might find there. His surprise was great when he could see Itosu sitting comfortably on a pile of dejected bodies and that he had taken care to put in such a position. Then Asato said to him: —*My friend, luckily, you're fine! I did not know this skill of yours and for a moment I thought about the worst. But here you are, more whole than me.*

From that place where he was sitting, he took his chin with one hand in a sign that he was thinking the answer and after a few minutes in silence said to him, looking into his eyes:

—*It happens that I am waiting for your diplomacy to control our attackers. Since I do not have such ability, I decided that it was best to request silence. And here you have them all as you see, very silent and unable to contradict you. Now can you explain your speech please?*

And saying this they started laughing so their laughter resounded throughout the environment and they were heard from a distance. They smiled in the projected image and smiled out of it sitting on the floor and surrounded by fog. Little by little, the cloud ring closed while the figures reflected there vanished. With one last look at the eyes they were silent. They understood then that this would be the last time they would see each other before Itosu finally transposed the doors of eternity. That was not an ordinary look and was impregnated with mutual recognition. For several minutes they contemplated themselves serenely and from their eyes each one tried to transmit to the other those codes of honor that had united them all their lives. Now from that position where they were kneeling face to face, there was a last greeting of always, with a *shomen ni rei* (greeting forward) supporting both hands and them foreheads on the floor, in an unmistakable gesture of respect and gratitude.

CHAPTER 2

MATSUMURA SOKON

The image of his beloved friend Asato Anko was diluted between the dense fog. He got up and started walking towards an area where the silhouettes of men who were at the time in the *Shikina-en* Park were emerging. This garden that was located to the southwest of the Shuri's Castle was used as a royal residence. It was on the banks of the large pond that there was where the *keimochis* used to train. The palace building was near one of the banks of the water mirror. The beautiful wooden structure was used for the entertainment of the royal family and important guests, preferably from Imperial China.

Suddenly he could see himself walking down those wooded trails, as he approached the two stone bridges that connected to a small island in the middle of the water. A small hexagonal pavilion was on a second island. The low and artificial hills that surrounded the small lagoon gave the garden some more panoramic observation points. And he continued walking until he reached one of those hills where he sat comfortably in *seiza,* to be able to contemplate the scenes that began to show with greater clarity. No doubt they were the royal guards and who instructed them was the same Matsumura Sokon, the great *Bushi* of the Ryūkyū Kingdom.

He could recognize himself among the guards who were there. At that time he was a young man of about sixteen and his Master Matsumura was about fifty years old.

He could still remember how he had joined the royal court as secretary and interpreter of King Sho Tai[9].

And had been his great friend Asato who would take care to exalt his virtues before the king himself and he accepted and made the necessary arrangements for his incorporation.

---

[9] It was the last of the kings of ancient Ryūkyū Kingdom. During his rule, which lasted just over thirty years the first public schools were created and the first telegraph line linking was founded Shuri with the rest of the islands.

But who would be more impressed by his ability to fight would be Master Matsumura.

And that memorable day was the one that appeared before his eyes in the scene that was being shown to him. They were making the application of the technique of one of the *katas* that the great master instructed. Standing at the center he asked his pupils to make a circle around him. The practice had to be done in the following way: according to Matsumura Sokon they were looking into their eyes and they were placed in *kamae* (on guard) face to face, they had to attack or defend themselves against some of their attacks. Although to show the technique it was tried not to produce injuries or damages of physical type, one worked with true rudeness. Must not forget that they were warriors and therefore they should be measured in combat to know their strengths and weaknesses.

The *Bushi* of the kingdom had an imposing figure. Despite his maturity that was already evident in the gray of his hair and beard, his physique was still a harmonious mass of muscles and fibers. When his eyes focused on a rival or enemy, his keen, penetrating gaze resembled that of an eagle or a falcon lurking for prey. And it was not in vain that he would have earned the fame with which he was known throughout the kingdom and even outside it.

He also had a leader's charisma that conquered the will of his *keimochis*. It must be remembered that they were brave men and very difficult to master. Certain codes not written but by everyone known indicated that their obedience would only be subject if the person giving the order was not a man of honor to whom they should respect. And in such a case Matsumura Sokon greatly exceeded that requirement. His example of tireless warrior, his countless feats and his way of maintaining calm even in very difficult situations, meant the appreciation and consideration of all.

And he started with an attack on one of those who formed the circle that morning. The subject was so surprised by the speed and precision that ended up giving noisily with his back to the ground. Immediately another of the chosen ones went out to attack him with a very violent *mae gueri* (front kick) but Sokon swept the other leg and ended up sharing the same fate as the previous one.

Suddenly, he noticed that the master put his eyes on his so that he could literally feel it as if they were two arrows. The dust that lifted the heavy fall of the body of the *keimochi* that preceded it was still floating in the air.

But there was no room in that place for doubt or for any hesitation. When Sokon chose someone, there was nothing left but to respond promptly to his demand.

Suddenly he came upon him, launching his attack with fury and speed.

He started throwing a *tsuki* with the fist of his left arm in order to use it as a distraction and immediately threw from behind a *mae gueri* and a *tsuki* with his other arm.

It was a throw from which there were not many possibilities of evasion, much less when the person who executed it was Matsumura. Then he remembered what his first *Sensei* taught him to give him great flexibility. Without thinking about the movement but unconsciously, he moved to the side and evaded his blows with precision and elegance. And there he was on the side of the body of the master who at that moment involuntarily gave him his vulnerable flank. He only showed that he could have counterattacked. That was also noticed by Sokon and by all those present who were surprised and speechless.

Now the grand master spoke and he said to all:

—*Today you have learned a great lesson and it has been provided to you by someone who is new to this guard. Until I attacked him, none of you knew how to measure the opponent's ability. You can not respond to a force if we have the power to do it is less than that. But if removed the impact target, then it will not matter how large it is. Without an objective to apply a force does not matter the power that is allocated to it. This is the correct application of tai sabaki[10]. Always remember this in future*

---

[10] *Tai sabaki* is generally used to prevent an attack, so that the recipient of the attack ends up in an advantageous position and is often erroneously called evasion. An example of *tai sabaki* is to 'get out of the line' of attack using *irimi* and *tenkan* movements instead of 'moving against' the attack. This implies the use of harmony instead of physical force. *Tai sabaki* is related to *ashi sabaki* (foot work) and *te sabaki* (hand work). Source: Wikipedia.

struggles. You must know each other and know your enemies or you will lose the battle.

From that day he earned everyone's respect and Matsumura began to observe him with different eyes. At that moment he could not see why, , but as he completed his preparation he understood that a legacy was being developed for him. Each day he gave himself more and more to be worthy of the consideration with which he was treated by him. He remembered that it dazzled him to hear and learn from this great master everything he taught him. He stood up again on that hill because the fog slowly returned to occupy everything and silently resumed his march on that white and cloudy path.

LEW CHEW[11]

From the foggy coast could see the fleet of battleships that had made port in the old Naha (or Napa

---

[11] So it was called to Ryūkyū appeared in ancient records as Loo-Choo or Lew-Chew.

Riang). It was the year 1853 and for the first time the security of the kingdom was threatened by western forces. Commodore Matthew Calbraith Perri (1794-1858) was on board the flagship.

The scene was now in the moments before that disembarkation. There Itosu was part of a circle made up of other *keimochis* that surrounded *Bushi* Matsumura.

The guards were ready in case there was ever such an opportunity. In fact, all the training had always been geared to foresee what should be done in case the integrity of the king and the whole court were in danger.

The great master spoke to them in this way:

—*We are present today in the front of a group of American soldiers, who although they come in peace, do so with guns and firearms. We do not know this enemy and without knowing it, for each battle we win we will lose another one. The good warriors make the adversaries come to them, and in no way do they allow themselves to be attracted outside their fort. We will keep calm, because avoiding the fight against well-ordered formations and not attacking large battalions, constitutes the domain of adaptation.*[12]

They silently agreed to such words and everyone knew what they should do, which could be summarized as "docile but with clenched teeth". It had been established as a strategy that King Sho Tai was not going to be able to attend to the visitors, since he was a child and would pretend that at that time he was in delicate health. The entourage of visitors would be received by servants who would actually be undercover *keimochis*. The *Seiden* Palace was arranged in such a way that in the royal room located on the upper floor, there was a discreet back door that allowed an escape to the outside of the building. And there they hid the royal family. At the same time, the risk of being surprised at the exit was minimized by the existence of a secret passage that entered tunnels more than three kilometers long under the castle. One of the mouths of escape was at the foot of a cliff where there was a small boat to flee.

---

[12] "The art of war" by Sun Tzu.

Major Perry, after considering that he would not stop at the excuses of Ryukyu's officers, mounted an act of controlled provocation. When disembarking from one of their ships, two heavy guns were dragged by some thirty sailors. They also landed about fifty officers with their sabers, leading two companies full of marines with rifles and bayonets. In addition, Perry was moving in a palanquin prepared for the occasion, carried by eight Chinese servants, as if he were a true Shogun.

And with this kind of arrogant parade, he headed towards Shuri's castle. When they reached the front door and saw the weapons, after a certain strategic delay, they were allowed to access. Once admitted to the palace, a group of Americans found a magnificent building, but it was practically deserted.

There was only the Regent Sho Taimu[13], three ministers and almost a dozen assistants. They were escorted to a large room in which the majority was composed by the Americans.

---

[13] Hereditary lord of the village of Mabuni south of Naha.

Both groups studied themselves while drinking tea accompanied by gingerbread. A while later Sho Taimu, invited Perry and his officers, to dinner at his house. After a tedious dinner, the Americans marched down the hill and took the rest of the afternoon to board the cannons. It was not long before Perry returned to Okinawa, but now he was much better received. And this was so by virtue of having signed an agreement on July 11, 1854, which was contemplated among many other topics: *"Whenever US ships enter any Port of Lew Chew, they must be provided with wood and water at reasonable prices, but if they wish to obtain other items, they can only be purchased in Napa."*

In the travel journals, Perry and his men said that during the entire time they were in Lew Chew they did not see a single weapon. That day in which they had to remain unarmed accompanying the ruler while they were surrounded by armed invaders, was recorded forever in the memory of Itosu. Not because of what happened, but because of what could have happened.

His master Matsumura had disguised himself as a servant and from there he observed all the arrogant behavior of the visitors.

The strategy of his martial mind told him that he should carefully compare the opposing army with his own, to know where the superabundant force was and where it was poor. When the invader had already left the port, they all met again and he said them:

— *War is a serious matter of the state; It is a place of life and death. It is also a path to survival or extinction, so it should be considered carefully. A victorious army wins first and starts the battle later; A defeated army fights first and tries to gain victory later. The best victory is to win without fighting.*

The great *Bushi* of the kingdom was a wise man and an excellent strategist. It was not necessary to risk the life or integrity of any of the members of the Castle in a reaction that could have had tragic consequences. After having recorded these moments of unforgettable teachings, he resumed his march along the misty paths that appeared before him

TSUNOTSUKI-USHI

After the great feat that Master Matsumura achieved, in which he named *Bushi* of the kingdom, the battles between bulls was gained greater notoriety in the whole island.

It must be remembered that on that occasion he managed to defeat a bull by facing him in a corral to which the animal responded fleeing in terror. Of course, his strategy was to attend daily before the fight to subdue him with a puncture in his snout. It was so then, the superb bullfighting specimen, recognizing who tormented him daily, fearfully decided to jump the fences of the barnyard and leave the site in a hurry.

Tsunotsuki means precisely facing two fighting bulls. Basically, the order of the fights is similar to the fight of sumo. As happens in this traditional art, the first clashes of *Tsunotsuki,* celebrate with young bulls, and the strongest bulls are scheduled to fight in advanced presentations.

Now he see himself walking down that street of the ancient Naha. The fog had dissipated but curiously at that moment he no longer watched the scene from the outside, but he was the one who starred in it. A gentle breeze hit his face, while on his lips he drew a slight smile. He knew that this place was very familiar to him because he could feel the same aromas and see those colors that he had once perceived. He thought then:

<This environment is familiar to me and I know I've been here before>

He had not finished formulating this affirmation when the scene appeared before him; he placed it definitively in the same moment and place that he evoked. It was a bull or *Tsunotsuki-ushi.* The breed is a "Japanese short horn" that traditionally has bluish-black leather. The magnificent and young animal wandered confused and very nervous, seeing that people ran terrified and in different directions.

He could then see at a certain distance, that one of the occasional passers-by who were walking down that street, he received a goring so strong that it resembled a leaf in the autumn with which it played a gust of wind. The poor man did not have any chance and the animal continued cornealing him on the floor. Someone had to come to his aid but everyone present was hiding out of danger. The only one who did not run or sneak was Itosu, who continued walking towards the animal. It saw him and began to run wildly to where he was with a clear intention to run over him with his horns.

People started yelling at him *<Run! Run! Save your life! Will kill you! >* But none of that happened, because he kept walking cautiously but with determination.

The witnesses who were witnessing the incident were dismayed, because despite the warning, the man did not attend to the cries that repeated tirelessly so that he could take cover.

What they did not know was that Itosu was preparing for the fight and that could be seen in his calm and open expression even if for them he was the road to certain death. Then the enraged animal charged against him, bending his head and shaping it to kill the impertinent intruder who stood in his way.

Flaunting his specialty that was the *tai sabaki* moved to one side while hugging the neck of the bull just behind his antlers. Taking him by the horns, he rotated his head, deflecting the animal's enormous strength and knocking it to the ground.

The people who saw the whole scene went from screaming in terror to a sepulchral silence. Once the dense dust dissipated they could see the brave man holding both horns forcing his neck so that the legs were in the air and he could not use them to standing.

The bellows and snorts of the bull did not stop repeating. But at the same time, it was beginning to get tired due to the stress to which he was being subjected.

Finally a couple of young *seko* who are responsible for supporting the bulls during the *Tsunotsuki,* came to their aid and tied the legs of the animal and then remove it meekly.

The feat of that day would be remembered forever in that village and little by little it would be extended to others until it reached the ends of the island. In silence, he was grateful spiritually for being able to live this glorious image again. And while he was thinking about it, the scene began to disappear and the whole painting vanished. When he returned to surround him the mist, only continued its transit towards the end along that misty path. He was not sure why, but he knew that many surprises would still await him on resuming that path.

UDE-KAKE-SHI

At that time in the mid-nineteenth century, the opening of imperial Japan to other horizons of world trade began to produce socio-political changes. The Satsuma clan, which controlled the archipelago militarily, enjoyed a widespread repudiation due to the oppressive and irrational methodologies with which they often treated the inhabitants of the islands.

It was a town of peasants and fishermen who were organized in classes led by the nobility established in Shuri. Their culture conflicted with that of Japan, while China's influence on its traditions and customs was notorious and significant. As for the series of rules that the king of Ryūkyū had to fulfill in front of the Satsuma Clan, they were established in a document called the *"Fifteen Precautionary Measures"*, which together with the two oaths signed in Kagoshima in 1611, detailed the economic and political restrictions on the kingdom. Trade, foreign diplomacy, and travel abroad were prohibited by the Clan.

 Ryūkyū's extensive trade relations with China, Korea and Southeast Asia, became interests for Satsuma and laws were created to prevent contact between Japanese and inhabitants of the kingdom.

The adoption of Japanese customs by Ryūkyū, as well as trips between the two islands, was also restricted.

As also, trips from Ryūkyū to the foreigner in general and receptions of ships in the ports of the kingdom were severely limited with exceptions only for official trade and diplomatic trips authorized by Satsuma.

It was also established to limit the amount of Buddhist temples and Shinto shrines in the kingdom.[14]

---

[14] Source: Wikipedia.

And this was the political environment in which Itosu Anko lived. In that climate and given that the inhabitants could not express themselves freely; the externalization of contained emotions was often given as street fights between fighters.

For this reason it is necessary to point out that in most of the confrontations in which Itosu intervened, he did so mobilized by the need to express himself in a patriotic sense. The proud character of its traditions and ancestral roots, of all the Okinawan people, is manifested in a strong attachment to the land and its culture still recognizable to the present.

The cloudy path now began to open space in front of his person. At times he was confused because until now he had arrived and at every step the experiences were increasing in excitement and emotions. He had almost forgotten that he was walking the path to the afterlife. Only that before leaving, he returned to those events and places that marked him in his dedicated life.

That is why he returned to the youth that showed him with the fullness of those years, but in which he was motivated many times by impulsive reactions rather than reflexive decisions.

And this case was not exactly the exception. He was now quietly resting and dozing on a rock on the coast of Naha. The cool breeze of the sea came to him and the unmistakable sound of the waves breaking against the rocks. The squawking of the birds completed that magnificent coastal panorama. Without having been warned of his presence by some subjects who were just talking there, he could hear from one of them something that did not like at all:

—*If it were not for Bushi Matsumura the Te (Okinawan karate) of Shuri would not mean anything!*

To which another voice replied:

—*That's very true! There Te only serves for personal gain, while here in Naha we produce real fighters and not for barbershop. There is no one in Shuri who is capable of defeating our champion Tomoyose!*

It should be remembered that at that time there was also a certain rivalry between different styles of the budding Art. That added to the fact that in the City of Naha, disputes were held that were consented by the servants of order. More precisely in a neighborhood called Yamagataya, there was a rock called *Ude-kaki-shi* in front of which certain clashes between wrestlers were usually held. They were accompanied by an audience that bet as a way to support their favorites and leave high the pride of the style to which they belonged. Logically, the neighborhood of Yamagataya enjoyed dubious fame, because in terms of police control it turned out to be no man's land.

Many reputations were praised and others lost in such confrontations.

To be able to carry out one of the fights, you only had to place your hand on the *Ude-kaki-shi* rock. That meant the desire to measure up in combat with anyone who dared to do so.

So it turned out that there was always a candidate who without any delay began to throw his punches without there being any rules for that.

At that time the local champion was Naha no Tomoyose. He was a strong peasant who was invincible in all the struggles in which he participated. It was the year 1856 and the destination of Itosu was marked unthinkably by an unbearable humidity that affected his health and forced him to move to Naha where he could enjoy a somewhat drier climate.

After listening to that conversation he decided that he should do something about it and the next day he decided to go to the place where the famous fights were fought.

He approached the arena and could see the way in which a very strong man was defeating one by one the occasional contenders who dared to face him.

Then he thought:

<Perhaps this is famous Tomoyose of which the men of the coast spoke>

But people had started to retire bored to see that no rival had appeared to be a worthy opponent of the undefeated local fighter. He hurried to take a leap and place his hand on the rock in obvious action of wanting to fight.

And this gesture was enough for people to crowd around the sand again. Suddenly he had in front of him the huge and stout figure of that man who looked at him with defiant eyes.

But as big as the figure of that fighter was, he was slow to throw every blow. In one of those crosses he launched a *tsuki* directly into Itosu's face. But before he reached the middle of the distance, he had already received three magnificent and fulminating blows to the head.

The subject staggered for a moment and breaking his knees collapsed heavily on the floor being totally unconscious. Instead of keeping things that way, two friends of the defeated giant jumped into the arena with an obvious intention of ending the irreverent winner.

While they insulted him, they surrounded him and the first one that attacked was received with an *enpi* (elbow) in the jaw with which he literally cut his tongue in two and while he was falling he spit blood to the ground.

The other individual who approached from behind was hit with the heel full on his abdomen which broke him in half and fell almost unable to breathe.

Three precise and fulminating blows ended with magnificent local exponents and in a few seconds.

And looking now at the crowd that had remained literally speechless he said:

—*I have come here to defend the Shuri-Te that I heard there, they call it "show of barbershops". Is there anyone else who continues to hold these sayings and wishes to face me?*

And saying this, he slowly glanced at the spectators around him.

But great was his surprise when he noticed that from the crowd arrogantly emerged a colossal adversary much larger than the previous opponents.

And he while entering the arena he was breaking the linen shirt that covered him, revealing his body exploded muscles and riddled with scars that surely were marks of previous battles.

Itosu for a moment felt intimidated and while both put their hands on the rock *Ude-kake-shi,* they greeted each other. The enormous man was none other than Tomoyose himself.

He thought that he should end this fight as quickly as he could, otherwise he would be defeated. He had the surprise factor in his favor because the champion did not know about his attack and defense strategies. People went crazy and encouraged their champion while bidding on bets against him that gave him loser in ten against one. They were in *kamae* (guard) facing each other as they watched, when the magnificent fighter threw a blow to him with his left arm and straight to the temple. The haul was so strong that surely to hit could have killed a bear. But Itosu with *tai sabaki* left the axis of the impact, blocked the blow with a *shuto uke* (side of the hand) and turned the elbow of the surprised Tomoyose that broke. The creak could be heard as if a bamboo stick had been split. The arm of the champion hung disarticulated in two pieces, while this one shouted showing a face with frightful grimaces of pain.

The formidable local fighter of Naha had been defeated in a few seconds by the exquisite technique of *Te* de Shuri and by its worthy exponent Itosu Anko.

Moving his head from side to side as a sign of regret for having lived through this impulsive stage of his life and thereby damaging other people he stood up.

Although ashamed of these scenes, he could not help feeling the same sensations of exaltation of his already distant youth. And it was strange, because it generated adrenaline to him but at the same time he worried about recognizing himself violent in those passages of his life. Over time he learned to control impulsivity and transform his explosive and irrational nature into a state of expectant meekness.

He had practically devoted his whole life to being a guide on how to use Art for peace and not as a source of violence. The images rotated incessantly in his mind although he could not distinguish at that moment what each of them was about.

Suddenly again the light was indicating the path he should take. Walking determinedly but without haste, he went towards the cloudy space that awaited him.

CHAPTER 3

MAKIWARA

As he moved through that place where the only thing he could glimpse was the light that was reflected in front of him, turning very white to the fog and preventing any image from being distinguished, new memories were presented. It was his revered master Matsumura who had instructed him to harden his limbs so that he could use them as if they were swords. His words echoed as if he were speaking at that precise moment:

—*Anko, if you prepare your hands, your feet, your elbows and your knees in such a way that they behave like a weapon, your victory will not require many blows, but only one. Like the samurai sword that ends all fight with a single cut, so you must train your body when facing an opponent. Ikken Hissatsu (annihilation with a single blow) must be the goal. Remember this and train hard!*

He did this and trained for many hours each day by inserting fingers and fists into the vessels containing pebbles of different sizes. This exercise was practiced by all the *keimochis* who, in a very neat row, passed from container to container, sinking their fingers and hands in a repetitive oscillation.

But he demanded much more than the rest of the entourage. Then he was looking for new ways of doing this practice. In addition to the advice of his master, he influenced him a lot when he was a boy, when his father punished him with the stick until he ended up facing him and disarming him. He knew that it was possible to defend oneself only with his hands even against blows made with a *bo* (stick).

But for that he must be very well prepared and have fists and forearms hard as a rock. And for that reason he trained using stones. He thought that only when he got to be as hard as them, would their hands stop feeling the pain present in such workouts.

He was hitting rock against rock to feel the magnitude of the impact that was required between the two to be able to break one of them. And he set out to be like the hardest of them.

The first thing he set out to do was to harden his fingers that already showed callused thanks to the work in the vases. But he thought that a strong fist needed harder fingers.

Then he devised a very particular way of training the firmness that had to be achieved by closing the fingers to get a solid, monolithic fist.

Near the house that he lived there was a small forest. There were different species of plants and trees. There was also a set of bamboo poles that rose many meters above the ground.

Bamboos can be small plants less than one meter long and with stems half a centimeter in diameter, although there are also giants: about twenty-five meters high and thirty centimeters in diameter.

Standing in front of this herbaceous formation, he used to measure the diameter of each cane by wrapping it around with his fingers, so that his thumb would always remain in contact with the index finger. And this was the maximum thickness he used to train.

He started with the thinnest sticks and squeezed them tightly around with his fingers that turned out to be like iron loop.

It was so much the power that put in it, that it did not resign to continue until obtaining the crunch of the wood. When he had succeeded in crushing the thinner stick, he would go on to a larger one. And so he could break through thick stems of bamboo thanks to the tenacity of his grip.

At that time his close friend Azato Anko used to invite him to his house. He was delighted to be his guest because he had a place there purely for the training of fists and feet.

They were *makiwara*[15] nailed to the ground and others of hanging type. They were made of wood or logs covered by ropes in the area of impacts.

For Itosu, this place was like an amusement park and both spent long hours hitting endlessly and training hard.

---

[15] The aim of *makiwara* is check body alignment and force projection at the time of impact, favoring step muscle strength and adapt the body to impacts, especially in areas where the direct impact occurs and surrounding joints (wrists, ankles, fingers and toes, elbows, etc). Source: Wikipedia.

That was the reason why he was able to knock out a man no matter how tall or how strong he was. His body is massive, with broad shoulders, developed shoulders, muscular arms and huge callused fists. On one occasion he used as *makiwara* a wall of stone bordering his own house and that separated him from the adjoining dwelling. He had placed the sole of a slipper that, fastened to the wall, served to cushion his violent impacts. With stealth he was banging there so as not to worry his neighbor because he did not want to bother his attention. But since his enthusiasm for hitting was increasing, he forgot to take such precaution and his impacts began to break the slipper that ended up falling on the ground. But that was not an impediment for him to continue his devastating blows. On the other side of the wall his neighbor shouted to stop while he made great efforts to contain it as it rocked as if it were an inverted pendulum. But the concentration and the noise resulted in such a way that Itosu did not hear a word of the afflicted neighbor. With a tremendous blow the wall ended up collapsing and almost did not end up crushing the terrified man, who after the dust looked at him with eyes wide open so much that it seemed that they were going to come out of their orbits. Although at that time the shame invaded him for what he had done, a spontaneous smile appeared on his lips, recalling the face of his neighbor's astonishment. Moving his head to both sides, he said to himself: *<Impetus of youth and immaturity that were part of my life>*

But he had learned that it is good to encounter difficulties in youth, because he who has never suffered has not fully tempered his character. Then he abandoned the image of that young Itosu repairing the damage caused and rebuilding the wall. And as that vision became blurry, he resumed his walk back to the light.

CHŌCHIN

His determined but unhurried pace along that diffuse path led him gradually to recall different sections of his life, some of which he almost forgot, lost in time.

His passage to the next life required him to be at peace with all those issues that once disturbed him or left him with marks.

The inner voice told him not to live those things as if it were a question of accountability. Quite the contrary, returning to them was for the sole purpose of allowing him to be at peace by looking at them now from the perspective of him comprehensive maturity. And he was very pleased to have before him a new opportunity in each case.

Now again the surprise put him on a little street of old Naha. It had been a day of hard work, the sun began to fade and the first lights of *chōchin*[16] lamps appeared of a few bars that were at that time.

---

[16] The *chōchin* has a bamboo frame divided spirally wound. Paper or silk protect the flame from the wind. The spiral structure allows to fold into the basket at the bottom. The chōchin hangs on a hook in the top. In today's Japan, *chōchin* plastics are produced with electric bulbs as novelties, souvenirs and *matsuri* and events. The oldest *of chōchin* record dates from 1085, and one appears in an illustration of 1536.
Source: Wikipedia.

He decided then that it would be a good idea to enter one of them to have something to eat and drink before retiring to rest.

The scene was now presented clearly and he was carried away by that desire, when before entering to perform its mission he could detect by the side of his eye that a shadow was approaching him.

He turned to see what it was and saw a young man who, without saying a word, threw him a *chudan tsuki* (blow to the middle area). Unable to dodge the blow for the unexpected, he only hardened the abdomen in which the impertinent boy's fist literally bounced. Throughout his life he had many battles facing different combats. He was never defeated although his physique showed marks of the wounds he received several times. But he was still full of vitality and his trained muscles gave him an image that seemed invulnerable. And not only was his surprise on this occasion, but after receiving the impact, he immediately took the astonished aggressor on the wrist to immobilize him. The pressure of his fingers was of such magnitude that the young man was broken by half the pain.

And now, without letting go of his hand, he continued towards the interior of the bar, playing down the importance of what had happened. Upon he taking a location, a young woman appeared who, somewhat frightened, she offered him a drink.

Before taking the first sip of his glass, he brought before his eyes the face of the boy who was also very ashamed and said:

—*I do not know you and I do not know what you have against me to attack me like that. But what do you think if we have a drink together and we discuss it?*

He smiled as he remembered the expression on the young man's face but also the lesson that he could transmit with his act by not responding violently. He also spoke to him with wisdom advising him to abandon that wrong path. He had also been a young man and he could find teachers who knew how to direct him. So he gave back in this boy something that life had taught him. A grateful face went opaque until disappearing before him.

At times he did not realize that this was not a dream and that each passage was very real. As much as it would have been at the time it occurred.

But neither could he restrain himself from the impulse to continue his march. Again his footsteps were lost in the thick white mist.

NINJUTSU

Due to the convulsed stage of political transition that were going through the kingdom, previous to being absorbed by the imperial Japan transforming itself in the prefecture of Okinawa, there was some mobility between the inhabitants of both islands. The cultural barriers that were sustained for a long time by the Satsuma Clan, began to show less rigor. Many Japanese of the "big island" were curious to know aspects of the culture that lived in the archipelago. It was also known about the fame gained by excellent warriors such as Matsumura Sokon among others and the knowledge that there was regarding the mastery of certain techniques of kobudo (handling of ancient weapons). And this motivated some to travel with the excuse of a tourist visit, but with the underlying intention to learn and unveil some of the secrets jealously guarded in Ryūkyū. But there the Art was taught secretly and privately. It was not something that was shown openly for several reasons. First, do not generate resistance among the samurais, and second, do not show the techniques of warriors or guards. Sometimes they even used to hide the techniques within traditional typical dances in order to confuse visitors.

So it was not easy to learn something, even when moving and residing there as a citizen. On one occasion a subject who had specialized in stealth or *ninjutsu*,[17] practices traveled from Japan to the island of Okinawa in order to spy on the techniques of the great masters of art.

There was also vain pride in being able to use his technique and with it stealing, without being warned, very well kept secrets. That motivated him much more

---

[17] *Ninjutsu*, also known as *shinobi-jutsu*, and as *Ninpō*, is the Japanese martial art of espionage and guerrilla.

and it even gave him adrenaline to make fun of the teachers who would not be able to detect his presence.

On one occasion this kind of insanity by stealth led him to commit an act too bold. One night he managed to enter the house of the best friend of Itosu that was Asato Anko. Sheltering in the shadows of the night he had managed to enter the same room in which he was resting. Almost by way of mockery, he decided that this master upon awakening would notice that someone had been present there that night. For that, it would change the location of some objects. He was sure that it would be enough to leave his intruder trace on it.

But Asato heard a sound and saw a shadow moving. Reaching for his *katana*, he went out to chase the snooper. Jumping first through the house and then through the roofs, he finally got lost in the shadows.

The next day he met Itosu and told him what had happened that night. Asato had an explosive character. While describing the way he persecuted the intruder without being able to reach him, which caused him much anger, his friend could not contain the laughter.

Now he remembered that dialogue:

—I assure you, my friend, that I went out to hunt down the bastard and he narrowly escaped me. If I had reached him, I would have made him pay for such audacity with his life!

And while he was smiling at the angry face of his close companion, he said him:

—That is an error Anko. You should have greeted him and asked him what he wanted.

With what the face of his friend became even redder by the fury and he did not stop laughing. Few days after that hilarious day, he was resting in his austere room. The air was just beginning to get a little cooler, although heat and humidity always ended up bothering his health. For this reason he could not fall asleep and began to hear a familiar sound. A few soft scratches on the door he thought that it would surely be his *neko* (cat) that told him he wanted to enter the house.

He was not going to pay attention to this request, but he wanted to make sure that it was his pet and not the intruder who would visit his friend beforehand.

Shortly after having taken a few steps he saw the animal that was approaching him and it placed between his legs. He immediately found that the noise probably came from another source and peeked out the window.

He saw the guy who was dressed all in black and he had his head covered with a handkerchief. He saw the guy who was dressed all in black and covered his head with a handkerchief. He has been characterized in such a way that he easily became confused with the shadows of the night. Without saying a word, he stood in front of the entrance opening in the *zenkutsu dachi*[18] position, which he usually used when hitting the *makiwara*.

Suddenly with a loud *kiai* that rumbled in the silent night, he unloaded a fierce *tsuki* that went through the door and immediately took the snoop in his hand.

His fingers were like tongs and the man who tried to make fun of another great master in this time was mocked.

---

[18] It is one of the basic positions of *karate*, characterized by its stability and strength. A forward leg with the knee flexed in line with the toes and the leg left behind stays straight.

After a few minutes Itosu found that it had already been enough punishment so he decided to loosen the pressure of his fingers and let go. However the individual losing all kind of composure fled repeatedly shouting:

<This man is a demon! This man is a demon!>

He did not spend much time in the neighborhood to find out what was the reason why those cries were heard on the peaceful night. Also because they could still see the huge hole that was left in the door of Itosu's house. Now he remembered what the dialogue with his close friend had been after the incident that morning:

—Hello friend, it is said that last night you caught the guy who used to walk in the dark. It is also said that you took her arm and he ran screaming in terror. It is true? Did not you tell me anything that I did not have to use violence and it was better to greet him and ask him what he wanted?

As usual, Itosu was looking into his eyes and, before answering, rubbed his chin with his hand while shaking his head slowly. After a few minutes of silence he finally replied:

—You listened people say that I took he hand. That was a very clear action that wanted to greet him.

—So, what's this hole in the thick door of your house?

—Oh that? … I wanted to stretch my hand to say hello to the unknown. But I forgot that my door was locked!

Then, he could no longer contain the laughter and his friend responded in a similar way.

How much he enjoyed this unforgettable memory of that time in which he gave a lesson to the daring intruder. With one last look at that endearing scene of his life he returned to the path to walk calmly and without haste. Everything had turned fog and light again.

BANDITS[19]

He had become a recognized master throughout the island because of the number of struggles in which he had participated and in which he had always won. That added to being the most prominent student of *Bushi*

---

[19] Source: http://www.dojosanchin.cl/relatos/06.php

Matsumura and people knew that this master would not choose someone who was not up to his technical ability, his knowledge and his unwavering honor.

That is why many times they challenged him to fight for no reason. It was part of the culture that many young people without experience would like to measure with great masters, even if they were defeated. It was like an unhealthy exercise to take a beating for the audacity to challenge a martial arts expert, and then to feel proud of having been defeated by a great master. However, he had learned not to harm potential contenders, just trying to put them out of action using only a minimum of violence.

At that moment the memory led him to walk the streets of Naha. He could see behind the fog that was disappearing, that at that time there were also many people walking in that place. A group of peasants were sitting in front of a house where a small stage had been improvised in the gallery and three people were playing the *Sanshin*.[20]

---

[20] The *Sanshin* (literally "three strings") is a musical instrument of Okinawa, the Japanese *shamisen* precursor. Like a lute is covered

The sweet melody reminded him of those days when he lived in Shuri Castle, but now it sounded *Asadoya Yunta*[21] ("the song of Asadoya"), a popular song that implied a slight political criticism of the change of government on the island. From inside one of the bars, a voice that was familiar to him called him to enter. He was a friend who wanted to share with him a round of *awamori* while remembering the old times together. After an hour, he realized that the darkness was beginning to change and decided that it would be better to go home. He said goodbye to his friend and returned to the street. There was a full moon, but it was a cloudy night, so the clouds turned off their light intermittently. Suddenly, he was surrounded by three bandits who demanded his money, something quite frequent at that time without law and

---

snake skin, and three strings handle body. It descended from Chinese sanxian, introduced around 1390 the Japanese archipelago of Okinawa, center of the ancient kingdom of Ryūkyū. Source: Wikipedia

[21] Originally from the island of Taketomi, in the Yaeyama archipelago (one of the archipelagos that make up Ryûkyû). The lyrics are about a beautiful woman, Asadoya nu Kuyama, who rejected a marriage proposal from the local Japanese governor.

with very little police control. One of the subjects said to the other two with a serious voice:

—*If that bag that is as fat as your head contains everything in money, surely it will be a good booty.*

He quickly made an assessment of the situation as advised by his knowledge of the strategy. He could see that the subject leading the group wore a pair of *sai*.[22]

Only one of the other two carried a *bo*, while the third was unarmed.

At that moment, the words of his master Matsumura came to his mind like lightning: <*If you ever get involved in a multiple attack, focus first on the weapon they can throw and then on the other*>.

But soon they would see firsthand how bad their irreverent intention to assault him would be. He was a warrior and not an ordinary warrior, but one of the best. He had been trained by the best master and had put all his effort into learning what he had been taught.

---

[22] Its basic form is that of a dagger blunt but a sharp tip, with two long side protection ('hands saves' or *tsuba*) also pointed attached to the handle.

Everything happened very fast. Taking advantage of the fact that the sky darkened for a moment, he jumped and shielded himself from the *sai* behind a tree. The subject of the weapon was looking for its best angle while aiming it with the intention of throwing the sharp object. But with a thunderous *kiai,* Itosu grabbed the weapon and placed a violent *shuto uke* (side of the hand) directly on the nape of the neck that ended up breaking his neck.

The man who had the *bo* went next and discovered that he arrived too late to save his friend who lay on the ground mortally wounded.

He began to beat him with the stick, but Itosu was an expert in defending himself against that weapon.

He saw that the subject was preparing to launch his best blow, but it was at that precise moment that, with a whiplash in his wrist, he turned the *sai* that had caught the dead thief, as if he were a swirl. He was right in the decision. When the man started the loading action, he already had the sai tucked deep into his chest, dying in this place.

The other man, seeing all this, fled in terror. He lived long enough to be able to tell about this tremendous encounter, which contributed significantly to highlighting the enormous skill and mythical image with which finally Itosu would be known.

This memory angered him and he did not regret at all to have finished with this social scum.

He knew how to defend himself, but those people had no problem killing and dispossessing the unsuspecting peasants if necessary.

They were difficult times for all and it was very bad that a few using force and using the Art in an incorrect way damaged innocents.

Trying to regain balance, he returned to the luminous path.

His breathing had stopped being agitated and with a determined step he continued the march.

CHAPTER 4

SAYONARA[23] SENSEI

It was an ordinary afternoon and as he usually did, he went to the house of his *Sensei* Matsumura to keep him company. It was very special moments that he shared with him. Sometimes he found him pruning the trees or the plants that surrounded the small house and he kindly asked him to help him in that task.

It was the last decade of the 19th century and the great *Bushi* was very old but his lineage still remained intact. Those who did not know him would not have discovered that he was an old warrior, because everything in him was austere and devoid of ornaments. When concluding

---

[23] *Sayonara* (さ よ う な ら) is composed of two words of the ancient Japanese and is no longer used today.

然 様 (そ の よ う, さ よ う) - *sonoyô, sayo*, which means: you have to be, as it should be, if so … resignation

な ら ば - *Naraba*, which means: then … hope.

It is a word of farewell but we can feel a kind of resignation, thinking that life has its limits and try to see a further, a continuation of that parting with a positive feeling.

Source: http://unajaponesaenjapon.com/18369/sayonara.

with some task in which he collaborated, they knelt in *seiza* and shared a cup of *ryokucha*. They usually talked long hours about anecdotes from their master, which Itosu listened to very happy and attentive. That day he noticed that he was very tired and saw him shake as he had never seen him before. He hurried to help him and asked him to go and drink the tea, with the clear intention of not embarrassing him, but at the same time giving him the chance to rest.

—*Anko, I appreciate your loyalty and your patience with me. I know that you try not to notice my slower movements and awkward moments.*

—*Do not say that Sensei. You are an extraordinary man and I have not met anyone the same in all my life.*

—*Arigato ichiban-deshi (thank you principal student), but it is something that I have accepted and that you must accept as well. I am an old man and I realize that my time is coming to an end. In that case I would like to tell you a dream that I have been persecuting without being able to achieve it and maybe you can manage to fulfill it for me.*

—*You will say Sensei. I listen carefully.*

—You know that our Art is the result of the effort of many masters who have persecuted with honor to leave this culture a way of life. That must be our Art: a way of life. Although different ways of attacking and defending are present in the synthesis of katas, their ultimate object is in transcendence. It would not make sense that so many lives of compatriots have been extinguished in vain, without in the future being presented as live Art. Transcending dear Anko, it means that you can transfer what you learned to each of the young people of this country. When finally a choir of children is performing a kiai product of some technique, I will feel that my work was put in good hands. I'm sure you can achieve it!

—Arigato Sensei. That is how it will be and I promise you that I will do my best to carry out your honorable mandate.

No more words were necessary because that promise was sealed with fire in the heart of Itosu.

They looked into each other's eyes and from the kneeling position they greeted each other with a respectful *shomen ni rei.*

When leaving that house he could still feel the affection with which his master dismissed him.

That night it was not easy for him to sleep because the promise he had made resounded and resonated in his mind. But he needed to speak with him again to tell him not to hurry to deliver his legacy, because they still had a way to go together. He also wanted to tell him that he was going to show him that his dream was not so far away and that he was sure that he could see it fulfilled in this life.

In the morning he hurried to go back to his dear *Sensei's* house to talk about everything he had thought about at night.

He knocks on the door as usual, but this time he did not hear the grave voice of Matsumura that told him to enter. However the same entered, although he was struck by so much silence.

He hurried to go to the room where he left the old warrior resting. And there was his rigid and immobile body in unmistakable sign of having transcended to another life. He approached delicately to his face and could see a faint smile on his lips.

That, at the same time, he produced him a lot of peace, although he could not avoid that at that precise moment salty tears spilled down his cheeks.

Accepting the irremediable, he lit some incense and got on his knees. And so he remained an indefinite number of hours in *seiza* next to the inert body of his master.

As the clarity of a new day was made other people were entering that room and were placing on their knees at his side.

He could not see their faces and did not even know who they were. Nor was he interested in knowing, because he felt absent from everything.

As he breathed with his eyes closed he only managed to repeat tirelessly in his mind: <*Sayonara Sensei* ... *Sayonara Sensei*>.

The sadness invaded him again as he did that day, but before he could realize it; the light began to become much more intense forward on the path.

THE ERA MEIJI

Shō Tai was the last king before the definitive annexation of the archipelago to Japan in the year 1879 when the present Prefecture of Okinawa was created, ignoring if that was finally the will of its inhabitants.

The new Japanese government, which had deposed the Tokugawa Shogunate, wanted at all costs to integrate the kingdom into Japanese territory, considering that it was an important strategic bastion for the defense of the country.

In fact, what was perceived as a tragedy by the Okinawan people was the interruption of relations with China, to which historically they were deeply linked and the pressure exerted to impose there the imperial system that governed the other Japanese administrations.

The new government of the Meiji era undertook the change of traditions and ancient Okinawan customs of life, in order to impose the imperial system.

With this also began to inculcate the veneration towards the person of the emperor.

The suffering *uchinanchu* had no connection with the figure of the emperor Mitsu Hito. Until that moment, their only ruler had been the deposed King Sho Tai, whereby they were completely disoriented.

Another aspect resulted from one of the slogans of the modernization process of the Meij government. Under the slogan: "a rich country and a strong army" mandatory military service was then imposed throughout the administration.

But as soon as a rumor began to circulate that the central government intended to go to war against China, many were the young people who mutilated themselves or who fled to the other side to escape from it. With the new edict on the National Conscription, new Japanese soldiers originating in Okinawa also appeared, but they were frequently subject to discrimination and ridicule because of their dialect, incomprehensible to all the military of the other administrations.

Okinawa had retained its dialect, and it is easy to imagine all the communication difficulties that the local authorities had with the emissaries of the government and those of other regions, at the time of forming the administration.

The measures to eliminate the dialect were very rigorous. It is said that when schoolchildren did not speak Japanese, they were forced to carry out a poster, in which was written *hogen fuda* (dialect label). Fashion and clothing also undergo great changes. The people of the island had always dressed their own traditional costumes, but now its inhabitants were encouraged to use the *Yamato* style, following Japanese fashion.

The wars against China in Manchuria (1894-1895) and against imperial Russia (1904-1905) were victorious for the Japanese empire.

Given these facts, the majority of the Okinawans were invaded by a sense of pride in belonging to the new order established.

The inhabitants of Okinawa wondered what their identity was.

Regardless of the intellectual level, in all areas of knowledge and in all sectors, they asked themselves this question.

There were teachers who adapt to the new reality, prone to Japan and other teachers who wanted to remain firm with their traditions, more prone to China. And this sometimes generated a desire to imitate them and other times they were hated for it.

According to the experiences of each one, it was a positive value or a negative value. Over the years, the restoration of the Meiji government came to be animated even by the son of the last Okinawan ruler, Sho Jun, who was the spiritual leader of the "restoration movement".

In addition, the statement of Iha Fuyu (1876-1947), considered to be the father of the science of Okinawa, according to which "the annexation of the Ryūkyū should be considered, as a liberation to the slavery of the Satsuma", was a stimulus to get away from local nationalism, and hence the progressive orientation of the Okinawans made an "integration" with the Japanese.[24]

Another very important aspect resulted from the dissolution of social classes. The techniques of martial

---

[24] Source: http://www.clubkisoku.com/secciones/articulos?id=804

arts, which until that historical moment are transmitted in a private way to the best and most chosen, they began to spread in a more open way.

Since the nobility had to assume other roles in society, to provide themselves with financial sustenance, many masters had to do particular jobs and start teaching martial arts.

This is the political and cultural landscape in Okinawa towards the end of the 19th century and the beginning of the 20th century.

Understanding the historical context in which life developed at that time will help to better discern a series of circumstances that occurred with different martial artists. Itosu's effort to incorporate art into the teaching of schools will also be more appropriately understood.

BUN-BU-RYO-DO

There is an old proverb that has been extended to all martial artists and is called *Bun-Bu-Ryo-Do*. The synthesis of the meaning of this expression could be summarized in the ability to be prominent in education, as well as in martial arts. In other words, appropriately combine physical training with the development of the intellect. In another of the meanings this term is also referred to that individual who possesses such capacity.

And this was the definition that would most accurately describe the person of Itosu Anko. His father had instilled in him the learning of letters by reading the Chinese classics in addition to the calligraphy that dominated to perfection. Thanks to his knowledge he was able to enter the king's court as a scribe, later becoming one of his bodyguards along with his master Matsumura Sokon.

Towards the end of the kingdom and like the rest of the members of the court of Shuri, he had to find an activity that would allow him to make a living without renouncing the dignity of the nobles. The abolition of social classes and privileges that once enjoyed the nobility completely changed the social face on the island. Some began to engage in trade, others opened their dojos in martial arts. There were also those who made different types of crafts and there were even those who specialized in alternative medicine of Chinese origin, such as acupuncture and phytotherapies. In the case of Itosu, he was able to acquire a small printing press with which he made publications of different writings. This allowed him to get involved with the education sector by offering his services in schools and colleges. He collected poetry and made small compendiums that he commercialized between educators and students. But that did not mean that he would give up having his own practice in a *karate* dojo. At the end of the 19th century (1890-1891) during the medical examinations of conscription for military service, it became evident that those who had been practicing *tode* had outstanding physical conditions. It is said that the doctors were impressed with the physicists of some young people who had been students of the master Itosu. He started by teaching a few students privately. But he still resonated the promise he had made to his teacher Matsumura. He had to find a way to extend teaching to a larger number of students.

His concern would bear fruit in the year 1901 when he managed to teach at the Dai Ichi Youth School in

Okinawa, introducing karate for the first time in the *uchinanchu* school system.

Considered a "great expert in Martial Arts" *(Meijin)*, he was the true promoter of modern *karate*, since he modified the teaching of this art as an element of physical and mental formation.

At this time, Itosu changed the pronunciation of this Chinese term 唐手 (hand of tang) to the word *karate*.

The most emblematic contribution of Itosu Anko, was due to a historical fact that meant the passage of a class society within an independent kingdom to another of citizens belonging to the Empire of Japan.

KARATE VERSUS JUDO[25]

At that time he had to live a very significant event and then the narrow white path began to expand forward.

---

[25] Source: http://www.karateca.net/forum/pessoas-e-historia/itosu-yasutsune-by-yuchoku-higa/

The fog that accompanied him permanently dissipated and the bright white light gave way to the daylight that was flooding everything around him. Recognized for his great physical strength and for having always emerged victorious in many clashes with adventurers who were attracted by his fame, he recalled that when this story happens he was already about 75 years old.

At that time a policeman *"naichi"* (nickname with which they were known inside the Japanese police) mocked the Okinawan karate people saying that it was an insignificant art and could defeat any of them.

He was in charge of the official formation of physical education in school curricula.

This inappropriate comment from the arrogant Japanese police had upset him greatly and he decided that he should take action on the matter.

Without further ado he went directly to speak with the director of the university who was also Japanese. Then firmly but calmly he said:

—*I wish to tell you that I have heard the unfortunate comment of a policeman who despises our Art. I want to clarify that karate is not a sport and in its essence is a weapon to kill. Its use should be limited to a last resort and as a personal defense.*

But the director who had some esteem decided to mediate in the matter communicating to the mayor what was alleged by the teacher. The police officers were Japanese, mostly from Kagoshima, and the one who had started the debate was a cocky guy who was considered invincible.

Unbeaten champion in *Naichi's* Art predecessor to *Judo* remained unperturbed in his own sayings.

The one who at that time was chief of police, he taking the floor, said: *—I think that this would be a good opportunity to compare the art of Japanese Judo with karate -* To which he added *—I considered it very convenient to allow this fight to be held. In this way, the Okinawan people will forever recognize that the art of naichi is far superior.*

When such communication reached the ears of the old master, that the combat would be officially allowed, he gathered all his students and told them in a very formal and solemn way:

—*They will soon see karate in a real combat situation, and I have decided to face the judo expert personally. I will not kill him, of course, but I have to show the insiders that karate is the most dangerous and effective art that exists with empty hands. Therefore, I want all of you to be present.*

It was thus that the confrontation between the two great martial artists was experienced as a great event: karate against Judo. That afternoon they were all gathered and very expectant in the university campus. Hours before the battle began; the stands were already full of students, police and enthusiastic audience.

Japanese police and officers were not content to show their sarcasm against the Okinawan islanders since in addition mocked beforehand for what they thought would happen.

A sepulchral silence was made in the room when that venerable 75-year-old master came in to defend the honor of karate. But the Japanese were offended and thought they were insulting their great Judo champion and his victory would lose all merit if it was limited to beating a helpless old man. For this reason, the combat almost is postponed, and thus it would have been of not being public the tremendous reputation of Itosu. So after considering it and with some reservations, the expert in *Judo* finally entered the ring.

After the presentations the combat began. The *judoka* expert described a circle around Itosu, making mocking gestures as if to keep up appearances. The master with great calm, moved while keeping his eyes fixed on the Japanese's eyes. The elderly contestant was so relaxed that it seemed ridiculous, even to his students. Suddenly, the police came forward and grabbed the sleeve and cleavage of Itosu's clothes, but in the blink of an eye, the audience could see with surprise how the Japanese fell sharply on the floor. Itosu had connected his left fist deep into the solar plexus of the *judoka*, accompanied by a loud *kiai*. The young policeman was on the ground beside him trying to breathe with difficulty.

Everything happened so fast that the Japanese officers were speechless. They heard a single *kiai*, and saw their champion writhe on the ground.

Then, Itosu, calmly, leaned towards the fallen one and began to practice a technique of *katsu* (art of recovery). In a very short time, his wrinkled hands, stained with senile spots, made the *judoka* return to its normal state.

Then, he went to the area where his students were, and with his characteristic deep voice, which was perfectly heard by the silence that enveloped the audience, he instructed them saying:

—*Today you have seen what karate can do against the uninitiated in this Art. It should never be used unless there is no other resource. I hope that this fight and this lesson will be told to your future students and will be remembered forever.*

And when he finished saying this, he went slowly and quietly sealing the end of this event that entered the history of *karate* forever.

CHAPTER 5

ITOSU'S KATAS

By the year 1901, Itosu Anko was able to introduce *karate* into the physical education program of the *Shuri Jinjo* elementary school. At the time he thought that the techniques of *katas* were too dangerous to be taught to children and began by attenuating them. As a result of these modifications, He taught them *kata* as a way to block and hit. This allowed them to gain additional benefits from the practice, such as improving health and discipline, but without providing knowledge of the highly effective and dangerous fighting techniques contained in the *katas*.

In 1905, Itosu was appointed professor of karate at the *Dai Ichi* Prefectural University and the Prefectural University of Teacher Training. In 1908 he wrote a letter to the department of prefectural education that summarized his views on *karate* and requested that it be introduced into the curriculum of all Okinawan schools.

He could see his wish fulfilled when he became part of the education of all Okinawan children. Itosu was a great developer of *katas* and it is said that he took the *kushanku kata* that his master Matsumura had bequeathed to him and divided it into a series of five *pinan*. Itosu remodeled and simplified the *kushanku* in the five *kata pinan* so that each of them was included in each year of teaching in the schools. That is, he had planned a *kata* for each year of the total of five that made up the secondary formation in Okinawa. It also included many other fighting techniques and other *kata* present in the Shuri region at that time (*Chinto, Passai, Kushanku,* etc.). The word *pinan* means "quiet mind" or "peaceful mind." The original Okinawan pronunciation of the first ideogram is *"pin"*, while the Japanese pronounce it *"hei"*. The name means that once these five forms and their applications are mastered, the *karateca* can rely on his ability to defend himself in most situations. The *kata pinan* are often considered training methods for beginners and therefore are often undervalued by many experienced *karateca*.

The main reason for these *kata* to be seen in this way is the fact that they were established for the first time when Itosu was introducing karate into Okinawan schools.

Some say that the *pinan* are softened versions of the advanced *katas* and that they were developed exclusively for children. However, Itosu also taught them *pinan kata* their adult students. It is probable that he had developed these *katas* during a period of time with the pretension that they were a synthesis of the best methods practiced in the Shuri region. When *karate* was introduced to Okinawan schools it was natural that these *kata* were chosen because they were relatively short. This is probably the only reason why they were selected and has nothing to do with the effectiveness of the techniques they contain. The main difference between adult and child training would simply be a matter of focus. As mentioned above, the children were taught the *katas* as "block and strike" while the adults would receive instruction in all the methods contained in the *katas*, including projections, strangulations, immobilizations, etc. The three main Japanese styles of karate (Shotokan,

Wado-Ryu, Shito-Ryu) practiced today all over the world, perform the *pinan / heian katas*. The reason why the *kata* pinan is common to all three styles is because Itosu Anko appears in an important way in their lineages. Master Itosu together with Higaonna Kanryo, were the main teachers of Mabuni Kenwa (founder of *Shito-Ryu*).

The name "Shito" derives from the two characters used when writing "Itosu" and "Higaonna". Itosu was also one of the professors of Funakoshi Gichin (founder of *Shotokan*). It is doubtful that Funakoshi learned *pinan* directly from Itosu, since he concluded his training with Itosu before these *katas* were created.

Some sources claim that Funakoshi learned the pinan de Mabuni in 1919, four years after Itosu's death. Mabuni Kenwa, Funakoshi Gichin and Motobu Choki (who also studied with Itosu), were the main karate masters of Otsuka Hironori (founder of *Wado-Ryu*). As it has been said the word pinan means "calm / peaceful mind". The same characters can also be read as "safe from danger" in Chinese. In general, *Wado-Ryu* and *Shito Ryu* styles prefer Okinawan pronunciation. While Shotokan practitioners, prefer the Japanese pronunciation *heian*. The reason for this last is due to Funakoshi Gichin giving Japanese names to all the *katas* practiced in Shotokan. He did it so that the Japanese would find the names easier to use, to further separate the art from any of its Chinese origins and to recognize the development of karate by the Okinawans and the Japanese. Funakoshi Gichin also changed the suffixes *Nidan* (2nd level) and *Shodan* (1st level) so that the names reflect the order in which the *katas* are commonly taught. This means that the *heian shodan* of *Shotokan* is called *pinan nidan* in the other styles and vice versa.

There are differences in the ways in which the different styles perform the *pinan / heian katas* but the general pattern that remains is the same.

These changes are the result of the developments made by the founders of each style. In an article in the Japanese magazine *"Karate-do Monthly"*, the expert in *karate*, born in Okinawa, Kinjo Hiroshi wrote:

"... It was in 1908 when Itosu Sensei formulated modern karate. In short, the fact that Itosu Sensei established a

modern form of karate-do points to the coexistence of old karate and modern karate at that time ...”

The five *katas* are quite different from one another, as a whole they are similar in the use of fundamental techniques and are an important element for teaching. Both they and their corresponding *bunkai* (applications) are studied by the majorities of the schools and *dojos* of *karate. Pinan kata*, there are from *Shodan* (first) to *Godan* (fifth), which contain a variety of techniques and almost all basic positions. They are mainly demonstrative *katas* (*Hyogen-Kata*), and serve mainly for learning *kihon*, displacement, power, speed, etc.

PINAN SHODAN:

In spite of being the first *kata* of the line *pinan*, it could be said that it occupies the third place for its complexity, getting closer to *pinan yondan* (fourth).

The *embusen* (diagram) is simple and resembles an arrow projected forward. Hand techniques are used especially *shuto uke* (hand side) and standing. Also hit with fingertips.

The characteristic of *bunkai* is the work of intermediate distance, this being the most privileged.

PINAN NIDAN:

The techniques are the most elementary. They are easy, but if they are not practiced well, you can not learn more difficult techniques. You have to repeat them many times until you can retain it perfectly. The *embusen* is very simple and looks like an arrow but this time with the vertex backwards. It also has the characteristic of resorting to shortcuts to the lower zone. The *bunkai* of this *kata*, bring out the art of combat preferably in the long distance.

PINAN SANDAN:

It has infrequent techniques such as fingertip strokes and flapping with the elbows taken at the waist that show its origin of the *kung fu* style of the "real cranes". This *kata* must be repeated and it is very important to learn the characteristics of these techniques. In the *bunkai* the short distance is used and applications of attacks to the vital points are found.

PINAN YONDAN:

The *yondan pinan* is very similar to the *shodan* because both use similar basic techniques. Especially hand techniques, also standing techniques. Open hand techniques indicate the Chinese origin of this form. The *embusen* is a bit more complex than in the other *kata pinan*. Comparing within the *katas pinan*, the *yondan* is the one that most uses standing techniques.It also includes varieties of *hangeki* techniques (defense and attack at the same time). The *bunkai* combines all possible distances of combat.

PINAN GODAN:

Almost all forms of elementary *tachi kata* enter into this *kata*. It is remarkable that it contains techniques of expansion and contraction of the body. It also contains defenses and attacks of short and medium distance. In the *bunkai* is the first *kata* in the series that provides applications of a slightly more advanced level.

An interesting note on the theme of the *pinan* offers an okinawan *karate* authority: Hiroshi Kinjo. He stated that Miyagi Hisateru (a former student of Itosu, who graduated from the Okinawa prefectural school in 1916) said that when he (Miyagi) was studying with the great master Itosu, he only taught the first three *pinan* with real enthusiasm, and that the last two were rather careless.

However it turned out, it could be stated that the authorship of the series of these five *katas* surely belongs to the master Itosu. In addition to the adaptations of other *katas* that he received from his master ancestors.

THRESHOLD

The master continued his steps along the luminous path that had accompanied him throughout all the scenes he managed to remember.

He was grateful in his mind for those significant passages of his life and the opportunity to look at them from the perspective of his sensible maturity.

He found that he no longer looked young like at the beginning of the road. Although the fog was still floating and his state of weightlessness and well-being was the same, he realized that he was reaching the end.

When he saw himself again and for the last time in the room where his body was in eternal sleep, he was already moving away from there. Silently, he left that place and could see that the light was with him, but with each step he disappeared behind him.

It was as if now he only had the possibility of looking towards the light, since there was nothing left but darkness behind him.

But it was a pleasant surprise when they began to emerge beside the luminous path, the cherry blossoms that he loved to admire in the *hanami.*

He then thought: <*What a beautiful vision the road gives me. I can see the sakuras (cherry blossoms) and perceive their delicate aroma*>. He was surprised at this magnificent contemplation of nature when he continued to see that the road stretched forward and began to show behind the fog, a huge ornate portal.

When he approached this image, the fog dissipated and then he visualized more clearly the white door that was there.

It was made of very fine wood, decorated with reliefs that represented different symbols, some of which he could not identify. Towards the sides, a pair of columns of red-gold color, made him supposes that they were the bases of a *torii*[26].

After admiring the beauty of that entrance, he was able to verify what was written there and, when approaching it, he managed to distinguish it with greater clarity. It was his name that appeared engraved on the wood and from there came the source of light that had accompanied him throughout his journey.

---

[26] A *torii* (鳥 居) is a traditional Japanese arch that is usually found at the entrance to Shinto shrines, marking the border between profane and sacred space. Source: Wikipedia.

Then he understood that this was the door that would take him to the beyond. However, when he tried to open it to transpose the threshold, it was not possible. And a voice inside told him he still had something to discover before leaving. Immediately he saw a black shape in the gloom, approaching him defiantly. He could not see his face nor understood very well what this presence was about, so he immediately warned him:

—*Stop there and tell me immediately who you are!*

—*I am the shadow of your fears and you must defeat me before crossing the threshold.*

The master then remembered everything he had learned. That the most important quality of a good warrior is to calm the mind to discern what he thinks and understand how the opponent he will face will be.

—*I'm ready and I'm not afraid so you'll be defeated.*

And while saying these words, he knew that he had no more weapons than his hands, while his rival wielded a sharp *katana* (samurai sword).

As usual, he tried to normalize his breathing. He knew that a noble man must wait for the most appropriate moment to give the best blow, but in a state of absolute calm. And that was what he had set out to achieve at that moment. One of the main teachings of the *Bushidō* Code (or Samurai) is that in order to keep the mind calm, one must keep in mind the idea of death at all times. Being prepared for the worst is the best weapon against fear.

It must be remembered that in the samurai code that laments the death of someone close to death is not like that. That death, if it had arrived alone, could respond to different motivations. But, above all, to the atonement of sins and the correction of errors: something that can only result in the common good.

And this was recorded in the spirit of Itosu and there was nothing to disturb him. He was prepared for death and there was no fear that he could defeat him. Then he could see before his eyes how the black shadow began to dissipate when he said him desperately:

—*How is it possible for you to defend yourself in this way? I realize that you will manage to defeat me and I will not have any chance to attack you.*

Unperturbed despite the claims of that formidable enemy that must face all the human being, he saw the dark contender disappear without remedy.

He was a warrior and this time he did not need anything other than his spiritual calm in front of the irremediable, in order to defeat that colossal adversary.

Immediately he saw that everything had returned to the previous state in which the shadowy warrior appeared. But he could see that the light that accompanied him all the way was almost extinguishing.

Before its brilliance disappeared completely, an image began to be projected inside a large ring of clouds. The scene that was presented to him was happening at that precise moment somewhere in his beloved Okinawa. He thought it was probably a school, because there were many children with their *karategis* that shone with their whiteness. From a dais there was a man who spoke to that same group of students. Maybe it was some professor.

Then he began to listen to what this educator was telling them:

—Dear students, we attend this day to an act of homage to a great master of karate-do. He honorably devoted his life to the teaching of art so that all of us today can know the techniques and through them be better people. That great teacher was called Itosu Anko and in his memory we are going to perform all together one of his katas.

Finishing saying this, the *kata* was announced to which all the children responded in chorus. With each account they made the movements concluding with a shrill *kiai* that they repeated in unison. A strong applause from all those present and the spontaneous laughter of the children resulted in the closing of this emotional tribute.

He could no longer hold back his tears and crossing his arms over his chest he dropped to his knees.

Then he said to himself:

< Now that I am old and tired I come to discover that I am nothing but the result of the love that I have been able to give and receive in this life> -While his mind kept repeating—*<I kept my promise dear Sensei Sokon... there you have your kids shouting at the Art in a kiai >*

He stayed like that for a few minutes contemplating that beautiful painting that life gave him in his last moments. As he moved his head slightly in order to affirm even more his thought, the image began to fade and found that the circle of clouds began to close until it disappeared completely. Suddenly and before he could get up, he heard the unmistakable sound of a door opening.

He stood in front of her that now enveloped him with a light that came from inside as if inviting him to enter.

And so it was that although he had not yet finished wiping his tears, looking inside he saw his *Sensei* Matsumura who was waiting for him with open arms and a wide smile on his lips.

Then, his face that still expressed the emotion of what had happened a few moments ago now became that of a grateful and smiling face. He no longer had any doubt that the time had come for his departure.

And with a firm and determined step, he crossed the white threshold and went forever to immortality.

PRECEPTS[27]

As has already been said in a timely manner in 1908, Itosu wrote a letter summarizing his views on *karate* and explaining why he believed it should be introduced into Okinawa's education system. Here that letter will be reproduced, and the ten Precepts registered in it. It gives us a vision of *karate* as it was when the master Itosu was taking him out of the shadows to become an Art practiced by millions of people.

There are different English translations of this important document; but unfortunately they vary greatly and it is difficult to determine which ones are correct.

It is logical that there is some variation in passing text from one language to another, but nevertheless some of these variations are not simply different ways of saying things, but often express very different feelings. Most of these translations are also made by martial artists. It is

---

[27] Source: https://borhshotokan.wordpress.com/2015/05/20/los-10-preceptos-de-anko-itosu/

also logical to assume that it may be that, unintentionally, they are putting their own views or opinions on karate into translations.

There is a little-known book from 1938 compiled by Nakasone Genwa called "Karate-Do Taikan". This important text contains material from teachers such as Funakoshi, Mabuni and Otsuka. It also presents relatively good quality photographs of the Itosu's letter of 1908.

The translation of the Itosu letter is copied complete below:

Karate did not develop from Buddhism or Confucianism. In the past the Shorin-ryu school and Shorei-ryu school were brought to Okinawa from China. Both schools have strengths and therefore the ready without embellishment.

空手道 は, 古代 中国 思想 (孔子 の 教 え) で
ある 儒教 や, 古代 イ ン ド 発 祥 (釈 迦 開
祖) の 仏 教 か ら 出 た も の で は あ り ま
せ ん. そ の 昔, 中国 よ り 昭林 流 と 昭霊 流
と い う 二 つ の 流派 が, 琉球 (沖 縄) に 伝
え ら れ た も の だ と 聞 い て お り ま す.
こ の 二 つ の 流派 は そ れ ぞ れ 特長 が あ
り ま す の で, こ の ま ま の 状態 を 大 切 に
守 り な が ら 伝 え て い か な け れ ば な り

ません. そのためには, 自分だけの思惑で, 型に手を加えないという心掛けが肝心です. それで空手道の修練の心得とその効用を, 項目ごとに行を改めて書き記してみます.

1. Karate is practiced not only for your own benefit; It can be used to protect your family or your teacher. It is not designed to be used against a single aggressor, but as a way to avoid being hurt, using your hands and feet, if on occasion we had to deal with a villain or ruffian.

空手道は, 個人としての体育の目的を果たすだけが, すべてではありません. 将来主君 (国) と親に一大事が起きた場合は, 自分の命をも惜しむことなく, 正義と勇気とを持って, 進んで国家社会のため, 力を尽くさなくてはならぬ, という名分を持っております. ですから, 決して一人の敵と戦う意図はさらさらありません. かような次第ですから, 万一暴漢や盗人から仕掛けられても, 平素の修練の成果により, なるべくこれをうまく捌いて退散させるよう仕向けることです. 決して突いたり蹴ったりして人を傷つけることがあってはなりません. このことが, 本当の空手道精神であることを, 強く肝に銘じて欲しいものです.

2. The purpose of karate is to make the muscles and bones hard as rock and use hands and legs as spears. If children begin training naturally in military prowess while in elementary school, then they would be suitable for military service. Remember the words attributed to the Duke of Wellington after he defeated Napoleon, "Today's battle was won on the playing fields of our schools."

空手 は, 専 ら 鍛 え に 鍛 え て 筋骨 を 強 く
し, 相 手 か ら の 打 撃 を も 跳 ね 返 す ほ
ど の 強 さ に す る こ と が 理想 で す. こ の
よ う に 理想 的 に 鍛 え 上 げ れ ば, 自然 と
何事 を も 恐 れ ず, 自 分 の 信念 も ま げ ず
に 振 る 舞 う, 逞 し い 行動 力 と 強 い 精神
力 が 備 わ る も の で す. そ れ に つ き ま
し て は, 小学校 時代 か ら 空手 の 練習 を さ
せ れ ば, い つ か 軍人 に な っ た 時, き っ
と 他 の 剣道 と か 銃剣道 の よ う な 術 伎
上達 の 助 け に な る 効用 が あ り ま す. 以
上述 べ ま し た よ う な こ と が, 将来, 軍人
社会 で の 精神 面 と 術 技 面 へ の 何 か し
ら の 助 け に な る と 考 え ま す. 最 も, 英
国 の ウ エ リ ン ト ン 候 が, ベ ル ギ ー の
ワ ー テ ル ロ ー で ナ ポ レ オ ン 一世 に 大
勝 し た 時 に い い ま し た. 「今 日 の 戦 勝
は, 我 が 国 の 各 学校 の グ ラ ウ ン ド 及 び
そ の 他 の 施設 で 広 く 体育 の 教育 を や

った成果である」と. 実に格言というべきでしょうか.

3. Karate can not be learned quickly. Like a slow moving bull, at the end will travel a thousand leagues. If one trains diligently for an hour or two each day, in three or four years you will see a change in your physique. Those who train in this fashion will discover the deeper principles of karate.

空手は, 急速に熟練しようとしても, なかなか難しいものです. 「牛の歩みは, 馬と比較して, より遅いけれども, 歩き続けていれば, ついに千里以上の里程を走破することが出来る」との格言があります. そのような心掛けで, 毎日一, 二時間ほど精神を集中して続けますと, 三, 四年の間には通常の人と骨格が違うばかりか, 空手のかなり奥深いところまで到達出来る者も数多く出るのではないかと思います.

4. In karate, the training of the hands and feet is important, so you must train rigorously with makiwara. To do this, drop your shoulders, open your lungs, increase your strength, grab the ground with your feet and focus your energy on the lower abdomen. Practice using each arm one to two hundred times a day.

空手 は，拳 足 を 鍛 える こと が 主体 です
から，常 に 巻 藁 など で，十分 練習 を 重 ね
る よう に 努 めね ば なり ませ ん．その
要領 は，両肩 を 下 げ，胸 を 大 き く 張 り，
拳 に 力 を 込 め，さら に 踏 まえ た 足 に
も しっ かり 力 を 取 り，吸 った 息 を 臍下
丹田（下腹 の こと で 古代 中国 思想 で 気 が
集 る 所）の ところ に 沈 める よう な 気
持 ち で 練習 する と よい でしょ う．ま
た，突 い たり，蹴 った り する 回数 は，と
も に 片方 で 百回 から 二百回 という と
ころ が 効果 的 と 考 え ます．

5. When practicing Karate positions, be sure to keep your back straight, lower your shoulders, put strength on your legs, stay firm, and drop energy to your lower abdomen.

空手 の 立 ち 方 は，腰 を 真っ 直 ぐ に 立
て，重心 の 平衡 が 崩 れな い よう 両肩 を
下 げ，力 が 体重 全体 に 平均 に 及 ぶ よう
な 心 持 ち で，しか も 両足 も 力強 く 立
ち，吸 った 空 気 を 臍下 丹田に 集中 さ せ，
上下 の 腹筋 も 丹田 に 引 き 合 わ さ れる
よう に して 凝 り 固 める こと が 大事 な
要点 です．

6. Practice each Karate technique repeatedly. Learn the explanations of each technique and decide when and how to apply them when necessary. Enter, counter, withdraw is the rule for torite.

空手表芸である形は，数多く練習した
方がよいのです．が，漠然と練習しても
それほどの効果はありません．練習の
効率をよくし，本物の技を身につける
には，形のなかにある一つ一つの技
（手数）の意味を正しく聞き届けるだ
けでなく，その技はどんな場合に用い
るか，ということを確かめて練習しな
くてはなりません．さらに，形の中に
出てこない特別な突き方（入れ）受け
方（受け）腕や襟を取られた時の外し
方（はずし）関節の決（極）め方（取り手）
などの高度な技があるけれども，それ
は秘伝になっておりますので，多く
は師が弟子に対して口で伝えるよう
になっております．

7. You must decide if karate is for your health or to aid

your duty.

空手表芸である形は，その技の一つ一
つについて，この技の目的は「体」即
ち体育（基本鍛錬）のために有効なもの
か「用」即ち実用（応用技）として練習
するのに適切であるか，あらかじめ
確実に理解し，目的と方法を確定して練
習しなくてはなりません．

8. When you train, do as you're in the battlefield. Your

eyes should glare, shoulders drop, and body harden. You

should always train with intensity and spirit as if you were actually confronting the enemy, and so naturally you'll be prepared.

空手 の 練習 を する 時は, ちょうど 戦場 に 出 かける ような 意気込み が なくて はなりません. 目 はかっと 見 開き, 肩 を 下げて, 体 に 弾 力 性 が つく ように 固 め, また, 受 け た り, 突 い た りする 技 の 練習 で も, 現 実 に 敵 の 突 き を 受 け, 蹴 り を 払 い, 体 当 た り し て い る 実 戦 さ な が ら の 強 い 意気込み で やらなく てはならないのです. このような 練習 を すれば, 自 然 と 他 ではまねのできな い すぐ れ た 成 果 が, 形 と なって 現 れ る もの です. 以 上 の こ と を し っ か り と 心 掛 けて 欲 しい もの です.

9. If you consume excessive force in karate training, this will make you lose the power of your lower abdomen and will be harmful to your body. Your face and your eyes turn red. Be careful to control your workout.

空手 の 練習 は, 自 分 の 体力 不 相 応 に, 力 を 入れて 気 張 り 過 ぎ る と, 上 気 して 顔 も 火 照 り, 目 も 充 血 して 体 の 害 に な る もの です. 以 上 の こ と は, どんな 視点 か ら みて も, 健 康 の た め 有 害 です の で, しっかり と 肝 に 銘 じ た い もの です.

10. In the past, many masters of karate have enjoyed long lives. Karate helps develop bones and muscles. Aids digestion and circulation. If karate were introduced, beginning in the elementary schools, then we will produce many men each capable of defeating ten assailants.

空手 に 熟 達 し た 人 は, 昔 か ら 長寿 の 者
が 多 い の で す. そ の 原因 を よ く 調 べ て
み ま す と, 空手 の 練習 が 筋骨 の 発 達 を
促 し, 消化器 を 丈夫 に し て, 血液 の 循環 を
よ く す る の で 長寿者 が 多 い と い う こ
と で す. そ れ で, 空手 は 自 分 以後 は, 体育
の 土 台 と し て 小学校 時代 か ら, 学 課 に
編 入 し て 広 く 多 く の 者 に 練習 さ せ て
い た だ き た い と 思 い ま す. そ う す れ
ば, お い お い 熟 達 す る 者 が 出 て, き っ
と 一 人 で 一 度 に 十 人 の 相 手 に も 勝 て
る よ う な 猛 者 も 沢 山 出 て く る こ と と
思 い ま す.

If college students training teachers learn Karate in accordance with the above precepts and then, after graduating, they spread it throughout the elementary schools in all regions, in 10 years karate will spread throughout Okinawa and the main islands from Japan. Karate will therefore a great contribution to our military service.

I hope seriously consider what I have written here.

Anko Itosu, October 1908.

右 の 十 ケ 条 の 意 図 で，師範学校 や 中 学校
で 空手 の 練習 を 行 い，将来 師範学校 を 卒業
し て 各地 の 小学校 で 教鞭 を と る こ と に
な っ た ら，そ の 赴任 に 先 だ っ て，十 ケ
条 に 述 べ ま し た 空手 教育 の 意 図 と そ
の 効用 を，細 か く 指示 し，各 地方 の 小学校
で も 不 正確 な 点 が 少 し も な い よ う に
指導 さ せ れ ば，十年 以内 に は，全国 的 に
普及 す る は ず で す．こ の こ と は わ れ わ
れ 沖縄 県 民 だ け の た め で な く，軍人 社
会 に お い て も き っ と 何 ら か の 助 け に
な る と 考 え，お 目 に か け る た め に 筆記
致 し ま し た
明治 四十 一年 戊申 十月
糸 洲 安恒

It is very interesting to note that the first line ("Karate did not develop from Buddhism or Confucianism.") he clarifies that karate is not based on Buddhist or Confucian principles.

Obviously Itosu felt that it was essential to make clear from the beginning that the Art he practiced was not a derivative of these religions or philosophies. This is important since some mistakenly see art in its entirety from Buddhist and Confucian perspectives. Followers of other religions may sometimes mistakenly lose their enthusiasm for studying *karate*, if they believe it is based on religious practices that go against their own.

Itosu tells us that this is not the case and that karate does not have a religious basis.

The Precept 1 contains the line "(the *karate*) is not designed to be used against a single assailant but instead as a way to avoid being injured using your hands and feet if we ever had to face a villain or ruffian."

This makes it clear that the original *karate* was not for a consensual fight against a single opponent or another *karateka*, but instead for civil self-protection. What works well in one area, will not necessarily work well in the other. Itosu obviously understood the difference between the two since he marked it in his first precept. As examples of these differences: closing the gap, clever footwork, guards, feints and varied combinations are common in a consensual struggle. But they are irrelevant to civil self-protection. And that is the reason why such methods do not appear in the *katas*.

When studying the *kata*, which is a record of the original art that Itosu is describing, it is necessary to make sure to understand that the *kata* was created to store methods for civil self-protection. When people see *kata* from a fight or combat perspective, it is when they misinterpret their nature and therefore come up with incorrect conclusions about how it should be applied.

A common example of this is when the *karatecas* make competitive "*bunkai* demonstrations" that begin with the antagonist in combat distance (that is, out of kick distance) as opposed to the extremely short distance associated with the actual combat.

Itosu was employed as a scribe by the last king of Ryūkyū and was very educated in the Chinese classics. After the dissolution of the monarchy, Itosu became a school teacher.

The highly educated Itosu also reveals knowledge of Western culture by attributing words to the Duke of Wellington in Precept 2. On the other hand, it is also interesting that Itosu says that the words are "attributed" to the Duke of Wellington. The quote "Today's battle was won in the Eton playing fields" is truly attributed to Wellington; but he did not say those words. It was actually several years after Wellington's death when the French historian and propagandist, the Count of Montalembert, attributed it to him for the first time.

Precept 4 strongly encourages the rigorous use of impact material.

Precept 6 proposes studying the *bunkai* or applications of the *kata* (ie, "Learn well the explanations of each technique") and personally explores the proper use of that *bunkai* in combat.

Many *karatecas* do not include *bunkai* in their training and therefore they are not training according to this principle.

Itosu also makes it clear that we must also decide when and how *karate* techniques should be applied. Even people who study *bunkai* often fail in this regard. Knowing what a *kata's* technics is for and knowing when and how to apply it effectively are two very different things. In the final sentence of Precept 6 ("Enter, counteract, retreat is the rule for *torite*") refers to the struggle (literally "grab hands") and is used in *karate* circles to refer to the struggle aspect of the original art. *"Torite"* was also an ancient name of *Ju-jutsu* and was used in that sense in some writings of Kano Jigoro (being Kano the founder of *Judo*). Itosu's rule of "entering, counteracting, retreating" would seem to be an anti-struggle advice, that is, when you are caught you can not immediately flee the scene, so go in, do damage, and then get out of there. It is sensible advice for civil self-protection and is totally in accordance with the nature of *karate* as explained in Precept 1.

The Precept 7 advises to decide if your *karate* is for the health or "to help in your duty" (that is to say, for its practical use). Perhaps the teacher here is making the difference between the health-oriented version of *karate* for children and the original combative art.

The Precept 8 advises to train in an intense and energetic way in order to be prepared for the severe and ruthless nature of combat.

This intensity when training is one of the keys to the true tradition of *karate.* In effect, this mental and physical intensity is more important than the technique. In the book: *"Karate-do. My way of life"*, Funakoshi, who was a student of Itosu, wrote: *"...Train with heart and soul without worrying about the theory. Very often a man who lacks the essential quality of complete seriousness will take refuge in the theory."*

We can currently see this "refuge in theory" and lack of intensity in some practitioners who claim to perform "traditional" training. To follow the true tradition, we would do well to remain faithful to the Precept 8.

The 10 Precepts of Itosu are unquestionably one of the most important historical documents about *karate*. To understand the *kata*, and the true nature of traditional *karate*, it is important to study the words and advice of the people who shaped the Art.

CHIBANA CHOSHIN

The continuator of the Shorin Ryu lineage was the master Chibana Choshin. He was born as the second son of Chibana Chohaku and his wife Nabi on June 5, 1885.

The family had a distinguished history and resided in the Shuri Tori-Hori village of Okinawa (now Naha City Shuri neighborhood Tori-Hori).

His family traced his lineage from a branch of the Katsuren Court and Choharu, Prince of Kochinta, fifth son of King Shoshitsu (Tei), but lost his titles and status after Mutsu Hito, the Meiji Emperor, banned the caste system in Japan.

His father sustained economically the family by making sandals and straw hats that he later sold to the peasants. So poor was the situation that Choshin could not finish high school because his arms were needed in the farm that had the family, at that time the only economic sustenance.

It is interesting to read from his own sayings his own biography:[28]

"The great master Itosu Anko studied Karate very hard. He was not only a great expert in Karate, but a scholar and excellent calligrapher. I first visited Anko Itosu in 1899 and asked him to teach me Uchinan-no-te (old name of Karate). On two occasions he rejected me, leaving me waiting at the front door. Only by asking him for the third time did he finally accept me as a personal student.

He taught Karate secretly in his house to a select group of approximately six or seven followers. They trained in Bu (karate as a martial art), not as a sport, as they do now. During that period of time I also kept my training a secret, even from my family. In 1903, or 1904, Itosu Sensei began to publicly teach Karate in the school setting. It was at this time that I told my parents that instead of going to school I had been practicing the art of "te".

In 1918 a group of Karate enthusiasts (Hanashiro Chomo, Kyan Chotoku, Miyagi Chojun, Mabuni Kenwa, Go Kenki,

---

[28]Source; http://www.karatebyjesse.com/chibana-choshin-butoku/

Oshiro Chojo, Yabu Kentsu, Kyoda Juhatsu, Yabiku Moden and me) formed a group for the study of Karate because the two better teachers had died. (Itosu Anko and Higaonna Kanryo , died in 1915).

His name was Karate (written as Tode) Kenkyukai, the one who settled in the city of Shuri.

This was the first time that practitioners of different methods (Shuri, Naha and Tomari styles) came together to train together and exchange information. Each time we met with a senior studen, we conducted him training and benefited from everyone's knowledge. This lasted until 1929 when, due to the popularity of this art, we all became too busy with our own students to train collectively.

I started teaching Shuri-te Karate-jutsu in 1920, but in 1929, at the age of 44, I opened my first training room (dojo) in the city of Shuri. In 1933, my good friend and colleague, Magusuku (Miyagi) Chojun, and I registered the names of our respective teachings with the Dai Nippon Butokukai (Great Martial Virtue Association of Japan). I called my teachings Shorin-ryu as the "small forest style". My colleague, Chojun-sensei, called his style the Goju-ryu which means "medium hard and medium soft style". We were good friends and he died in 1953. He was a good colleague and friend of all the Shorin practitioners. He is missed.

Both Bucho (Bushi) Matsumura and Itosu Anko were poor. When I talked about this to Itosu, he told me that this was not a universal truth, that a martial person is poor. He claimed that the Okinawa Bushi (warriors) were poor because they did not know how to handle money, as was the custom at the time.

A true martial artist from Okinawa earns a living away from martial arts. They should not worry about making money from teaching martial arts. A martial person must make a living away from martial arts so as not to contaminate it through the influence of "earning money" to "make a living".

This is the Okinawa way.

Karate, as it is transmitted, changes every few years. This is a common phenomenon. It happens because a teacher must continue to learn and add his personality to the teachings. There is an old Okinawan martial arts saying that Karate is very similar to a pond. So that the pond lives, it must have contributions. It must have currents that feed the pond and replenish it. If this is not done, the pond stagnates and dies. If the martial arts teacher does not receive input of new ideas and / or methods, then he also dies. He stagnates and, through boredom, dies of unnatural causes.

I remember learning the Tawada Passai (Passai / Bassai) kata from Tawada-sensei. At that time I received instructions from Itosu and he also taught a version of Passai kata which he called Matsumura Passai, which I learned.

In 1913 or 1914, having practiced Tawada-no-Passai with all my heart, as was customary at the time, I approached Itosu and informed him about this. He asked me to show him the kata. I did, and Itosu told me that this was the best execution of this form rarely seen and that he himself had witnessed.

Then he told me that this form should be preserved and passed on to future generations and added to their (my) teachings. Then (in Kobayashi-ryu) the Matsumura Passai is now called Passai-no-sho and the Tawada Passai is called Passai-no-dai.

Many of today's practitioners are too timid in their training. They train only with the idea of being able to finish and not with the idea of progressing, striving to improve. You must train hard if you want to progress; otherwise, you are a mediocre practitioner and there are many of them.

If you want to learn mediocre karate, go somewhere else and do not waste your time.

If a teacher teaches with his heart, he can only expect the student to train with his heart. It's fine, then, that both the teacher and the student progress. The student motivates the teacher and the teacher teaches the student the correct attitude and spirit of the Okinawan martial arts. This is a good training: the student and the teacher progress together!

When you train you must dedicate yourself only to the path of Karate, do not think about anything else. Do not think about others, or what they may think. You must develop the ability to focus your mind, hands and feet with strength. You must not only learn the movements of the body, but also the investigation and study of the technique itself.

You must develop and improve before reaching the age of fifty.

Your body begins to deteriorate naturally after fifty years of age, so you should adjust your training accordingly. If after fifty you still train every day, then you can not decline so much. I noticed a slight decline at fifty, but I do not think I have diminished much between the ages of fifty and sixty.

Of course, you can not avoid deterioration to a certain extent, but if you continue training you will not age so quickly, even between seventy and eighty years of age. Therefore, you must train continuously.

In the old days we trained in Karate as a martial art, but now they train in Karate as a gymnastics sport. I think we should avoid treating Karate as a sport, it must be a martial art at all times!

Your fingers and the tips of your fingers should be like arrows, your arms should be like iron. You have to think that if you kick, you try to kick the enemy who is already dead. If you hit, you must push to kill. If you hit, then you hit to kill the enemy (Ikken Hissatsu).

This is the spirit you need to progress in your training. The effort required is formidable, and you can force the body by doing too much. So keep in mind your own physical condition and train accordingly. Years ago I decided that through my own hard training I wanted to leave my name related to Okinawa Karate. I trained hard and learned the best I could. Now I think my name will remain a bit in the Karate do history of Okinawa. Not only do we need physical training, we have to think for ourselves, study and investigate the kata and its applications.

It is vital to understand the kata and train your body to develop the core of Karate. You can achieve a five or six times increase in the power of your body if you train hard. Naturally, if you do this, you will be satisfied with the result, so train a lot. If you become great, it depends on just two factors: effort and study. Your movements should be sharp, never be slow, and when you train a kata, your eyes will become sharper and your blocks and blows will become stronger. Even when you turn seventy or eighty you should continue your research with a positive attitude, always thinking "not yet, not yet ..."

EPILOGUE

Chibana Choshin died of throat cancer at the age of 83 years. He never stopped training. In many aspects, including economic, the life of Chibana *Sensei* proved difficult and exhausting, rewarded only in the satisfaction of seeing multiplied in thousands and thousands of people who today practice the *Shorin Ryu* style. In addition to being the only Okinawan *sensei* of *karate* who received the order of the emperor in the 4th degree *(kun-yonto)* for his merits in teaching and spreading the ancient art of *karate*. Heir to the *Shuri-te* tradition, he understood that Art leads to a profound study of man and does not end with his modern sports expression. Chibana modified the old *kanji* used by Matsumura, so *Shorin* (Japanese) began to read *Kobayashi* (Okinawan), which means exactly the same: Young Forest or New Forest. However it is possible that Bushi Matsumura had thought at the time, when he created his own definition of *Shorin*, which was also a way of paying homage to the three kings of the "Sho" dynasty he served.

Chibana was already contemporary to such consideration of his distant predecessor, for which his objective clearly was to differentiate it from the Japanese expression to make it merely Okinawan. Thus, its main students have maintained the modified *kanji* of *Kobayashi-ryu*.

Master Chibana had among his students Shimabuku Eizo, Ishikawa Seitoku, Nakahama Chozo, Chibana Akira, Ankichi Arakaki, Katsuya Miyahira, Yuchoku Higa Nakazato Shugoro, Shinzato Yoshihide.

His death on February 26, 1969, was the origin of different lines of *Shorin's karate*: Yuchoku Higa *Sensei* creates the *Shorin Ryu Kyudokan* line, Nakazato Shugoro *Sensei* the *Shorin Ryu Shorinkan*, Nakahama Chozo *Sensei* the *Shorin Ryu Shudokan*, Katsuya Miyahira *Sensei* the *Shorin Ryu Shidokan* and Shinsato Yoshihide *Sensei* the *Shorin Ryu Shin Shu Kan*.

On August 30, 1964, a monument in honor of Anko Itosu was erected in Furushima Forest, north of Shuri. It is a large stone engraved in front and behind in homage to the main driver of the *Shorin Ryu* and was commissioned by Choshin Chibana who was the only important direct student of Itosu alive at that time.

He took care to promote this project as an authentic homage to loyalty and pride.

The inscription penned by Choko Iraha and engraved on the stone by Ishimine Jitsuhiko, reads as follows:

"Itosu Anko was born in the small village of Gibo de Shuri in 1831. He died in the village of Yamakawa in March 1915, at the age of 85. Having mastered the principles of karatejutsu, Itosu Anko dedicated his whole life to the development of Modern Karate Itosu Anko is recognized as the man most responsible for taking Karate forward.

It closed the doors of darkness and introduced and systematized it in the school where it first served as a physical education complement. His contributions are immeasurable foundations in which modern karate was newly established. "

August 30, 1964

Dictated by Kobayashi-ryu Karate-Do Kyokai

President; Chibana Chosin

Calligrapher; Iraha Choko

Engraver; Ishimine Jitsuhiko"

Finally it can be said that the ancient *Shorin karate* path is still open for those who want to practice it seriously, with respect and with honor.

It is a knowledge that has no beginning or end. It begins with intense physical exercises, then continues with the applications to combat and concludes in an inner spiritual path.

But it is very important to recognize that this path has two great enemies: the size of the practitioner's ego and the failure to recognize the limits of their own ignorance.

This book was printed in the
month of October 2018 in
graphics workshops: Independent
publisher.